Books of Merit

A Perfect Night to Go to China

DAVID GILMOUR

A Perfect Night to Go to China

A NOVEL

Thomas Allen Publishers

Toronto

Library and Archives Canada Cataloguing in Publication

Gilmour, David, 1949 –
A perfect night to go to China : a novel / David Gilmour.

ISBN 0-88762-167-8

I. Title.

PS8563.I56P47   2005   C813'.54   C2005-900055-4

Editor: Patrick Crean
Jacket and text design: Gordon Robertson
Jacket image: Peter Urbanski Photography

Published by Thomas Allen Publishers,
a division of Thomas Allen & Son Limited,
145 Front Street East, Suite 209,
Toronto, Ontario M5A 1E3 Canada

www.thomas-allen.com

**Canada Council
for the Arts**

The publisher gratefully acknowledges the support of
The Ontario Arts Council for its publishing program.

We acknowledge the support of the Canada Council for the Arts, which last
year invested $21.7 million in writing and publishing throughout Canada.

We acknowledge the Government of Ontario through the Ontario Media
Development Corporation's Ontario Book Initiative.

We acknowledge the financial support of the Government of Canada
through the Book Publishing Industry Development Program (BPIDP)
for our publishing activities.

09 08 07 06 05   2 3 4 5 6

Printed and bound in Canada

For my wife, Tina Gladstone

A Perfect Night to Go to China

1

I never really got back to sleep after that. When the alarm went off a few hours later, I was already up, sitting on the side of the bed, my chin in my hands. I thought, I'm going to feel terrible all day.

I went down the hall to get Simon up. He'd kicked off his blankets and was sleeping with his arms straight over his head, as if he were diving into a deep pool of water.

I put my hand on his cheek. "Simon," I said, "Simon." I lay down beside him and almost dozed off myself. Just being near him settled me. I think I even had a dream, a small one, but then I shook myself awake.

I said, "Come on, we have to get up." But he was already awake, lying there with his hands on his chest, staring at the ceiling. It looked rather odd, a six-year-old boy with his hands on his chest. Like an old man or someone in a coffin.

I took him into the bathroom. At this time in the morning he couldn't aim straight, it ended up on the floor or the toilet rim, so I'd learned to put my hands on his shoulders, to point him while he took a pee. Then he gave a little shudder and pulled up his pyjama bottoms, never shaking quite enough so there was a little dark stain high up on his leg.

I said, "You should give it a slightly longer shake."

"Okay," he said.

I went downstairs and turned on the lights in the kitchen. It was still winter dark outside. I filled up the kettle, rattled around, doing this and that, but when I didn't hear anything coming from Simon's room after a few minutes, I went back upstairs and took a look. He was sitting on the floor, one leg in his jeans, staring into space.

I said, "Simon," and he jumped as if he'd been pulled from a dream. "What are you thinking about?"

"Nothing," he said and put the other leg in his trousers.

I was in the foyer putting on his snow pants when M. called. She was in Havana, selling a second-hand phone system. Thousands and thousands of used phones. She said, "I just wanted to hear his voice. Is he still there?"

I was tired all that day, a kind of grinding weariness.

I kept catching myself feeling shitty, thinking, Oh yes, that's what it is. And because I was tired and when you're tired you think of all sorts of ridiculous things, I found myself thinking that it was unfair that I'd gone to bed early and been punished for it. I might as well have stayed up to three in the morning drinking martinis with a lampshade on my head. Not quite, but you see my point. I thought, I won't do that again, go to bed too early.

So when I picked up Simon later that day, I was a little short with him. I said, "I'm not feeling good today so don't ask me too many questions, all right?"

He said, "Can we still get my doughnut?"

I said, "Of course. Let's just not talk too much about it."

By the time I got him bathed and washed his hair that night (those sleepy eyes staring at me), it was nearly eight-thirty. I said, "I'm too tired to read you a story, Simon. You'll have to look at the pictures yourself."

He said, "If you're tired, why don't you go to sleep?"

I was going to tell him that's what I'd done the night before, that's why I was a bit grumpy, but he'd have taken that as a willingness to negotiate.

I said, "Just because."

He put on his pyjamas and got into bed, hair still damp; I kissed him on the cheek and then, without

4

looking back, I closed his door. I said, "I'll turn your light off in a moment."

I tried to watch television but I couldn't keep my eyes open. I thought, It's happening again. I went down the hall, took a cigarette from the pack in the fridge and went out onto the front porch. I'd only been there a few minutes when I heard music coming from a bar down the street. I like live music, it excites me, like being close to a secret. I felt in my pockets and found a five-dollar bill. A lucky break. I opened the door to the foyer and listened for noise at the top of the stairs. Nothing, not even the rattle of the refrigerator.

I didn't put on a coat or boots, that would have made it too much of an outing. I just nipped down the street, the air frosty and exhilarating, snow piled up fresh and gleaming on windowsills, car hoods, bicycle seats, even that little square bolt on the top of the fire hydrant.

It was a charmless little bar in Chinatown, you probably know it, old-style Formica tables, photographs of the regulars on the wall, waiters they found I don't know where. Hard to imagine those creatures with a life outside that bar. Even the air was oily.

There was an all-girl band playing in the main room. I'd seen them before; they were tough girls, fuck-you girls, and one of them, the bass guitarist, had a narrow cat's face and a button on her leather jacket that said, "Forget it." She smiled at me when I stepped into the bar. I don't know if she knew it was me or I was just another guy who kept turning up wherever they were playing.

A waiter with a red nose pointed me to a table. I said no. But I took a draft off his tray, staying close to the door. Then cat girl stepped up to the mike and started in on a slow ballad. *I don't know just what love is. Tell me you'll show me the way.* I had a feeling she was singing it to a woman at the front table.

I don't know how long I stayed, maybe fifteen minutes, but once I was back out in the cold air, hurrying along the sidewalk, I realized I'd gotten quite the little fizz from those two beers. Possibly three. Sometimes you do, sometimes you don't. The front door to my apartment was open and I remember thinking that was stupid, heating a house and then blowing it all out the front door. I ran up the stairs and into the kitchen. It was a pleasant feeling, as though I'd had a whole night out. I kicked off my shoes, my feet were cold, and thought, I'll run a tub of water, I'll sit on the side and dabble my feet in the hot water. Like sitting on the side of a dock when I was a kid. But first I went down the hall to check on Simon. I loved the way his room smelt, his warm little body. But his warm little body wasn't in the bed. It was gone.

I'm not going to go into all the details of what happened next. I simply can't go through it again and I'm sure you don't want to hear it, either. Let's just say this. The police came quickly, two, three cars, almost at the same time. They went up and down the street, door to door, knocking, talking, asking. Knocking, talking, asking. I went with them. A Chinese neighbour who barely spoke English said she'd seen a small boy standing on the porch from her third-floor window. His feet were bare. Standing out there in the snow. No shoes. Very bad, she waved her finger back and forth. Very bad. By the time she got downstairs, he was gone. Must have gone back inside. Her granddaughter translated.

That night you could hear a megaphone moving slowly along the snowy street, asking for information, a small blond child, six years old, in his pyjamas. A metallic science-fiction voice you wanted to obey.

A detective with greasy hair said, "I think there's a very good chance someone's looking after him." His partner kept staring at me.

M. flew home the next morning; there were no recriminations. I think she was afraid to jinx the situation by injecting poison into the air. Then more cops, stomping their feet in the downstairs foyer. Going back up and down the street, then doing the next block. Sometimes M. went with them; sometimes I did. Howard Glass telephoned. I said, I can't talk now.

Near noon, someone else came forward. A young man and his wife had just finished having dinner around the corner at the Shanghai Gardens; they were returning to their car when they saw a little boy standing on the porch of a grey house, calling for his father. Looking up and down the street, calling, "Daddy? Daddy?" He darted back inside when they tried to approach him. They thought about knocking on the door, making sure everything was okay, but they didn't.

A third detective, this one with an expensive haircut and a sleek green suit, said, "He must have come out again." M. sat motionless on the couch, as if this image, Simon standing in his pyjamas on the porch, had frozen her brain and she couldn't think anymore.

The cop with the greasy hair said, "We had a kid once; went across the street and fell asleep in an apartment. Eighteen hours later we found him." The cop with the expensive haircut shot him a look but it was too late. I knew that twenty-four-hour thing, that after that things get more . . . difficult.

A reporter from *The Globe and Mail* came by to pick up a photograph. You could smell the cigarette smoke on her; she must have butted it out just before she came upstairs. She said, "This'll help, this'll really help."

M. said, "We'll want that picture back."

"Of course," the woman said. "We're very careful with this kind of thing."

I saw the same photograph on the supper news that evening, a sandy-haired boy with sleepy eyes. It was a picture M. had taken a few weeks before, when he had a cold and stayed in his pyjamas all day.

Sometimes during that second day, when I was alone and absolutely still, I had a feeling that Simon was speaking to me, his small boy's voice whispering in my ear like he did when he slept in our bed. *Shh, Simon, sleepytime.* But I couldn't make out what he was saying. There was another sound, too, like shattering glass. Only softer. I couldn't tell exactly what it was.

So that night I waited till the police left and then I went out alone. I stood in the middle of the snowy street, I put out my arms and I waited for him to speak to me. The Chinese woman watched me from her third-floor window. I waited and then I waited some more. I felt myself drawn to the other end of the street, away from the bar. I headed east. I went two blocks and then I headed south. I said, I'll find you.

An hour later I was wandering along a footpath by the side of the road, cars whizzing out of the fog, when I saw a break in the guardrail. A snowy road led to the right. I followed it for a hundred yards and found myself in a field with small fires burning here and there in the wet air. Figures huddled around barrels of burning trash, getting warm. Scattered around were little shacks with flashlights and gas lamps behind the windows. In the distance you could see the great bridges of the city and hear the hum of cars roaring along them.

I went over to one of the burning barrels; there were six or seven people there, suspicious, unfriendly faces.

I said, "I'm looking for a child. I have a photograph here. Can you have a look?" A woman, my age, wrapped in a blanket, thin cheeks like she didn't have teeth, looked at the photo and said, "A little young, isn't he?"

Her buddies laughed, wrapped in sleeping bags, standing in front of the burning barrel. A dog lay against a cardboard house, some guy fixing the window with masking tape.

I said, "Where are we?"

The woman with no teeth said, "Queer Park."

There was another snigger. Somebody threw something into the flames. A young guy with a baseball hat, very serious face, said, "She's just kidding."

I passed the picture around but I had the feeling I shouldn't have, that these people were bad luck, that nothing ever good or lucky could ever come out of them, these ghosts among the trash cans. You could almost hear their jaws snap when you walked by.

A skinny guy with a beard looked at the picture and after hesitating a second, said, "Do you have a cigarette?"

I said no, I didn't smoke. You could feel his whole body go slack, the interest gone. He almost dropped the photograph onto the ground.

"You better let me have that back," I said.

By the time I stepped out of the light from the fire, the whole bunch of them had forgotten me.

I took a taxi home and set out again. *Be still, listen. Don't think so much. Just let him pull you.* I started around the block, stopping in front of half a dozen houses. I waited, I listened. Nothing. But then I felt it, that sensation when you've given up looking for something and suddenly, unbidden, you remember where it is.

I went up an unshovelled walk and knocked. A thin black woman answered the door. Grey hair around her temples. The police had already been there, she said. Twice. She looked behind me, out onto the street, to see if I was alone. Was I the father? Yes. "Could I have a look around?" I said.

Her face lost its friendliness. "I told you. The police already come."

I said, "You're Grenadarien?"

"Don't matter where I'm from."

I pushed past her. A black man and three children were watching television in a living room off the hall. The door partly open. She said, "See here, I *live* there. This is my house."

I stood at the foot of the stairs. I said, "Who lives up there?"

"What you mean, who lives up there?"

I went up to the second floor; there was a door just to the right of the railing with an unusually low doorknob. I tried to turn it. Locked. I listened carefully. The man came up the stairs after me, taking them two at a time. I said, "Don't fuck around with me."

"Nobody fucking with you. What you doing going through the house like that?"

"Who lives in there?"

"Gone," he said. He waved his hand. "Back to Grenadier."

"I know Grenadier," I said. I wanted to soften him up. "I used to go there all the time. My mother lived there."

"Me not give a shit where your momma used to live."

"You're standing too close to me," I said.

He didn't move; I could feel him trying to get within range.

I said, "Back up. I mean it. I know what you're going to do."

"Then quit my house."

A police cruiser pulled up beside me when I was back on the sidewalk. It was the detective with the greasy hair. He said, "How you doing?"

I said, "Okay."

He said, "Got a minute?"

"Sure."

He said, "You want to get a coffee?"

I said, "I'm kind of busy."

"This won't take long."

We went to that doughnut shop on Spadina where the bank used to be.

"People say cops always eat doughnuts," the detective said. "They think it's some kind of a preference thing."

"What can I do for you, officer?"

"It's just what's open. You don't always want to be eating just hamburgers. The cholesterol'll kill you. You want something light, break up the monotony a little."

"Your job gets monotonous?"

"Dealing with assholes gets monotonous." He took a bite from his doughnut. "I like these ones. With the sparkles on top. But you got to be careful. They're bad for you, too." He looked at the doughnut for a second and then returned it to the plate. "You can't just go into people's houses," he said. "It's against the law. Besides, you could get hurt. Some black guy thinks you're shaking him down."

"Right."

"No," he said, showing some steel underneath, "I mean it. You can't be doing that again, okay?"

"Okay."

"Because if you do, I'm going to have to lock you up."

"Lock me up?"

"For your own protection."

"All right."

He looked at me carefully.

"I got it," I said.

He kept looking at me. "Yeah?"

"Yes. I got it."

He dropped me off at the corner of College and some street. "Remember what I told you," he said. "I don't want to make a bad situation worse."

"I will."

When I got back to my apartment, I saw one of Simon's little red sandals tipped on its side in the middle of the hall. M. hadn't wanted to move it. I stepped over the little shoe and went up the stairs to the bedroom; I knocked on the door; she didn't answer. I went in; I could see a red coal in the darkness. She was lying on the bed.

"Where've you been?" she asked softly. You could hear she was getting hoarse from all the smoking.

"Looking around."

"Is it still snowing?"

"Off and on."

"Any calls?"

"Uh-uh. Nope. No calls."

I watched the red coal move tow   her night table. She said, "Do you remember that song he liked so much, the one you used to sing to him in the tub?"

I thought for a moment. "The one about the bird?"

"Yeah."

"Sure."

"I can't remember the last verse," she said.

I sat on the end of the bed. She moved her feet so they weren't touching me.

"I've been lying here trying to remember the words," she said.

"I can't either."

There was a long pause. "Yes, you can."

"I don't feel like singing now."

"You don't have to sing. Just the words. Just tell me the words." The coal on her cigarette brightened.

I said, "*'Did your lady friend, Leave the nest again.'*"

"That's right. That's the one." She turned her body toward me, as if to get closer to a fire. "What then? What's it say then?"

"*'That is very sad, Make me feel so bad—'* I can't remember what comes next."

"Please."

"*'You can fly away, In the sky away, You're more lucky than me.'*"

She let that hang in the ashtray of I couldn't see but I had a feeling her lips were moving, t... she was saying something. The coal went bright red. Then she said, "What's the matter with you, Roman?"

"What do you mean?"

"Just tell me. It would help me."

I took an involuntary gulp of air. "I made a mistake."

I slept for a few hours on the couch. It must have been near morning; I could hear birds chirping in the snowy branches. I dreamt about my mother, who had been dead for many years. She was wearing the red scarf. It was Italian silk and she used to wear it to parties.

In my dream, I said to her, "*You* don't have him, do you, Mom?"

"Of course not," she said. "I've never even laid *eyes* on him."

The snowplough roared down the street again. I got off the couch and with the blanket trailing behind me went upstairs to the bedroom. I stood in the doorway and when I heard M. stir abruptly I said into the dark room, "I know he's alive."

"How do you know?" she said.

"Because I can hear him talking."

"What does he say?"

I said, "I can't make it out. But I know it's him."

"Is he safe?"

"Yes."

"Are you sure?"

"Yes. I am."

I went back downstairs and lay on the couch. It was just getting light over the bar at the end of the street. I closed my eyes, I listened. Nothing. I thought, He must be sleeping. I could see him under a blue blanket. If you looked very closely you could see the blanket rise and fall, just a bit. It was him breathing. Breathing slowly. I said, "I'll find you." Then I went to sleep.

My boss telephoned that afternoon. He said, "How long's it been?"

"Thirty-six hours." It'd been a few hours longer but I couldn't bring myself to say it. By his pause you could tell what he was thinking, but he didn't have the manners to charge through it, to keep talking. Even now he wanted to show off, let me know how much he knew about police procedures.

He said, "Take all the time you want."

I thanked him. I had a strange, disconnected thought. I suddenly understood that disease, the one where people make their children sick; it's like being a child yourself, the way people look after you.

I went out again that night. Garages backlit like Hollywood sets; bushes like hanged men; windows bulging like eyeballs; a third-floor bedroom painted a childlike red. I looked in garden sheds, in parking lots, in backyards. I whispered his name down dark stair-wells. I said, "Simon, are you there?" A dog chased me from a back porch, snarling, pulling on a chain. A drunk staggered out of the darkness at me. I peered into an abandoned car. Nothing, not even a sensation. I tried to feel him, not to think him, but I kept wondering, Where would *I* take him? Fifty-eight pounds. Where would you go? It had to be nearby. But when I stopped in front of a house or started up a driveway, I could feel a sort of invisible door close. As if he were whispering in my ear, No, not here. Keep going, keep moving. Was I hearing his voice or just remembering it or just want-ing it? He was slipping away from me. I said, "Don't go, Simon. Don't go."

It was the middle of the night when I got home. The bedroom door was shut. I went into my study. I pulled out my diary; I flipped through it: all those entries about women, how much I hungered for their bodies. It was like the diary of a man with an eating disorder, a man who couldn't stop dreaming of chocolate éclairs. It made me queasy, the dull-wittedness of it, the myo-pia. I skipped ahead, more of the same, more and more and more, but I couldn't stop reading, I couldn't close the book because, on all those pages, during the time they were written, Simon was *nearby*, he was down the hall or he was in the tub or he was asleep in his bed, and by reading those pages, I could feel those hours when he was close by. I even sniffed the pages. But it was old paper. I went into his room and picked up his pyjamas, they were draped over his bed, and put them to my face. I remembered dreaming about my mother in her red scarf, my mother dwelling in the land of the dead, sleeping till noon, the ghosts of old bankers and roués sitting around her bed, chatting. She would know everyone in town, my mother, all the newly arrived dead. If she hadn't seen him, he wasn't there.

I rose from my chair to tell M. but I heard, or thought I heard, a door slam with such force that you could almost feel the breeze. *Don't do that!*

I let it slip to Howard Glass the next morning when he came by. Even as I said it, I knew it was a mistake. "I feel like sometimes he's talking to me."

"I believe in those things," Howard said with a shrug, a gesture meant to imply that all things were possible. But they're not all possible and he didn't believe me and I sensed, at the very back of his thoughts, like a man in a hat, a kind of personal exoneration. Another competitor retired from the field. I thought, How evil we are, how deserving of unhappiness. Everywhere I looked I saw loathing. I saw it in the faces of the detectives when they came to the door; I saw it in my neighbours; I saw it in M. when she didn't think I was looking; but I didn't protest. I thought, More. Give me more.

And there was: more policemen kicking the snow off their boots downstairs; a different reporter, then another who forgot her address book on the coffee table and had to return to the apartment to get it. The relief on her face was palpable. All those addresses, all those phone numbers possibly gone.

I heard the megaphone moving down the street in the middle of the night, that comforting metallic authority, as though God were looking for him, as though God were saying, You better hand him over. But then they didn't come again. I thought, They've gone somewhere else to look. You just can't hear them from here.

I saw a news crew shooting the front of our house; they did a long pan starting at the bar on the corner, coming to rest on the porch. Then they did it again, a safety as we call it in the business. I was glad to see them. Only that morning I'd wondered, was it my imagination or was there a slight cooling down in the attention paid to Simon's vanishing? The police, the newspapers. They're not getting used to this, are they? To him being gone? It was as if (and I kept this to myself) M. and I had been standing in a crowd of kind, smiling strangers but somehow that crowd, still warm, still kindly, had moved, almost as if it were a single mass, slightly *away*, so that now there was a space between them and us.

When an old movie theatre collapsed in midtown, killing two contractors, it made the front page. I thought, This is bad, this is distracting. I shut myself in the bathroom later that day, it was snowing again, I sat on the toilet, I closed my eyes and listened. It took a while. There was the clank of a water pipe, a honk from the street, someone locking their car, the thump of the clothes dryer, but beyond that, beyond even the snow falling, I could hear him, I could hear him speaking to me. But he seemed farther away, alive, as alive as before but more distant. I thought, It's the snow. It's interfering.

When I came out of the bathroom, M. was standing at the kitchen window, looking out at the small park below us. "Do you think the snow will make it harder to find him?"

"No," I said. I put my hand on her shoulder but she moved out from under it automatically, not even taking her eyes from the window.

2

A few days later, I saw a picture of Claire English in the newspaper. She was an old girlfriend, a baby-faced woman with short, wispy hair. I thought, She's looking well after all these years. Must be doing well, too. A big picture like that in the city paper. I read on a bit, what she'd been doing since I last saw her: publicist for a small literary press, government liaison officer, campaign assistant, executive assistant, deputy minister's press officer, not a backward step the whole way. But why, I wondered, was everything in the past tense? Then I looked at the top of the page. It was the obituary column. She was the star of the day's dead. Claire would have liked that. She was ambitious, always looking for the next bump-up. Death by ovarian cancer. I remembered what she'd said to me the first time we slept together. I was eighteen. "I've just made love to you,"

she said, "and I don't love you." Seemed then, seems
now a bit harsh.

I went to her funeral the next afternoon. I didn't
know why, I just had a feeling I should. It was an over-
cast afternoon, the snow sitting in sullen mounds. You
could see the first black flecks collecting on the tops of
the banks. Reassurance that worse things lay in store.
Riding in the taxi, I looked this way and that. I'd never
noticed before how many small children there were
in the city. Little clumps of snowsuit waddling up the
street, holding a parent's finger or staring into a snow-
bank. Their parents pulling them on. One woman had
her toddler on a leash.

I got to the church just before the service started.
There was a handful of people outside I hadn't seen
since university; they were older, paler, greyer and fat-
ter. Everybody seemed to be going to pot, but maybe it
was the sunlight, that flat, sunless winter light makes
everyone look like they're in a Bergman movie. Staring
out a church window, waiting for God.

I saw Johnny Cotton. He was a good-hearted drunk
in college and I could see from his paunch, from his red
eyes, that he was still a good-hearted drunk. He gave
me an authentically hearty handshake, said my whole
name twice over in that bass voice of his. There was a

time when Johnny was a handsome young actor working all over town. He said to me one night in a bar, a hint of bewilderment in his voice, "I'm going to be a big star, Roman. I'm going to be a big fucking star." He ended up training attack dogs on the west coast, his own company, he said. Not a trace of defensiveness. Now he was back in town, doing a bit of drywall, even a bit of acting. Who knows? He didn't know about my son and I didn't tell him. A good guy but not much of a newspaper reader, I guess.

I ran into Jeremy F. there. I knew him from my days working in public television; a tall, elegant man, late fifties, looked like Philip Roth. Didn't matter what was going on, Jeremy always landed on top. Change of government, change of party leader, he was always on the right side. People who admired him said he was like Canadian royalty. His presence, his style. To the people who liked him slightly less he was an apparatchik.

"I'm so sorry," he said, looking me right in the eye. And for a second I understood how he had done so well with his career. Because he meant it. He *was* sorry. Didn't matter that he'd forget about me in ten minutes and enjoy an expensive lunch. "Call me," he said. "I'm at your disposal."

I said sure. I meant it, too, even though I knew I'd call his office, he wouldn't be there, his secretary would take my name, and he'd never get back to me. Because I didn't have anything for him. It wasn't personal. There were just so many hours in a day and only so many useful people in it.

All the way through the service I kept looking over the crowd, back and forth, like a cop driving through the city. Looking for what, though? Why was I there? Claire's teenage daughter went to the altar at the very end and addressed the congregation. Beneath her, a level below, a blow-up of her mother, the one in the paper, when she was in her late twenties. The daughter was pretty, with a red blush of life in her cheeks. She read a letter to her mother. Several people cried. Dabbing their eyes and looking on. I kept looking over the crowd. The young girl said, "And Mommy, I promise I'll remember how beautiful you were. Not how you looked when you died." Which, quite frankly, struck me as a rather odd thing to say.

Later, when I came out of the church, I ran into Jeremy F. again. He was smoking a cigarette.

"Quite the service," he said and raised his ample eyebrows. Man to man, as if we were both suffering in our own private way but not making a fuss about it.

I said, "Indeed."

He said, "Last year, I went to Larry Epstein's funeral. You knew Larry?"

"The politician."

"He had two kids, and they both spoke. Now *that* was something." He talked about it as if it were a competition, who had had the saddest funeral. Larry had won, apparently.

I said, "I've got to be off," and shook hands and even then I hesitated, wondering if I should stay around a bit, talk. It irritated me that even in those circumstances I was worried about people liking me, whether I was making a good impression on them, whether they'd speak well of me when I was out of sight.

When I got home that night, I stepped over the little red sandal and went up to the bedroom. The room was dark; a red coal at the top of the bed.

"Why don't you kill yourself," she said.

"Then we'll never find him."

A few hours later, the smell of cigarette smoke woke me on the couch. M. was standing above me, silhouetted against the window. Dark blue flush of dawn.

"Why do you keep saying that?" she said.

"What?"

"That you'll find him."

"Because I will."

She considered that for a second. You could feel she was torn. "You can't crack up on me, Roman," she said uncertainly.

"I'm not."

"You think we'll find him?"

"Yes, we'll find him."

"But where is he?"

"Someone has him. Someone saw him on the porch and took him."

"Do you think——?"

"Yes?"

"You think if they took him, they took him for his own protection?"

"Yes."

"So they'll be nice to him?"

"I'm sure of it."

"But people do such bad things, Roman."

"Not all people."

She stood there, cupping her hand under her cigarette so the ashes didn't fall on the carpet. "It's true. Not all people are bad." Hesitating. Then: "Still, if they're not bad people, why don't they return him?"

"They don't know us."

"Can't they see how much we're suffering?"

"Maybe they're not looking."

"Right," she said. "Maybe they're not looking." Then she went back upstairs, still holding her hand under the cigarette.

I dreamt again that night about my mother. We were walking down the main street in a humid Caribbean town. Daytime. It must have been near lunch, the street was jammed, men milling about in white shirts and trousers, kids selling cigars, laundry hanging from the balconies overhead. Today Mother was wearing a floppy hat, which suited her, and sunglasses. Tanned, as always.

"You see that white building," she said. "Ernest Hemingway lives there."

"Really?"

"You sound surprised."

I said, "I would have expected something more elaborate."

"It's a very simple place," she said matter-of-factly. "A white room with white walls overlooking the harbour. Utilitarian is the word. Shall we go up?"

I hesitated. "Maybe he's working."

"He's used to people dropping in." She looked at me coolly. "You're not a very curious fellow, are you, Roman?"

"I'm not here for that, Mother."

"No?"

I said, "There's something I've been meaning to ask you."

"Uh-huh."

"Is there anyone *new* in town?"

"Of course."

"Anyone I know?"

"You're being coy, dear," she said. "It doesn't suit you." She stopped under the red awning of a bar and looked inside. A stocky man in a sleeveless white shirt was opening up, straightening the tables, chairs.

I said, "Mother, listen to me for a second."

"I am. I am."

I said, "I'm looking for an old girlfriend of mine. Short hair. Not very tall."

"What's her name?"

"Claire English," I said.

"Your father had an eye for short women, too. I thought sometimes he should have married a doll."

"Is she here?"

"She caused quite a flurry when she got off the bus. All the men. But I don't have the foggiest idea where she's staying."

"But you're sure she's here?"

"Yes, but I haven't met her yet, if that's what you mean." Fanning herself with her hand. Waving at a short man across the street. "Don't tell me you've forgotten who that is?" she said.

"Who?"

"That's Jerry Malloy."

"But he looks fine."

"They can do anything here, Roman. It's just a question of knowing when to stop asking for things." She gazed again into the shadows of the bar. "Let's go in for a moment, Roman. I'm wilting. It's so pleasant before the music starts. After that, my God, you can barely hear yourself think."

"Was there anyone else on the bus?"

"What?" She was halfway in the bar now.

"Was there anyone else on the bus with Claire English?"

"They don't come by bus, dear. Those days are long gone."

"But stay, Mother, stay just a little longer."

"No, dear, I simply can't take another second of this heat."

I woke up on the couch; it was four o'clock in the morning. I could smell cigarette smoke upstairs. Footsteps moving around the house, as if M. had lost something and was looking for it. I fell back asleep with a craving to return to my dream. And I did. It was like a movie resuming after a reel change.

It was nighttime now in the Caribbean town; music poured out of the bars. I spotted my mother coming up a narrow cobblestone street with a group of people I knew from my childhood, Dr. Frum, our dentist, Gloria Styles, Johnny Best, the red-cheeked boy across the street who'd committed suicide.

"Roman," Dr. Frum said, "are you still wearing your retainer? No point in your parents paying all that money to get your teeth straightened if you don't wear your retainer."

"It's in my drawer," I said. "I put it on every night."

"He shouldn't keep it in his drawer, surely," Gloria Styles said.

"As long as he doesn't break it, it doesn't matter *where* he keeps it," the dentist said. Everyone had a good laugh about that.

We stepped up onto the sidewalk as a group of partiers passed by wearing hats and blowing horns.

"A busload of engineering students," the dentist said softly.

"How sad," I said.

"They'll settle down," Gloria said. "Everyone's like this the first week or two."

The street rose gently for another hundred yards through grand, decaying buildings, polished cars parked here and there.

"They have to wash them and wax them every day," Mother said.

"A good brushing takes two minutes," Dr. Frum said. "They don't take their teeth seriously until they're gone. *Then* they come to me."

The street funnelled into a crowded, noisy square; people squeezed together, shoulder to shoulder, just their heads moving about. A handsome young man with black hair and a military jacket nodded to me. I thought, Where could I possibly know *him* from? At the other end of the square a large cathedral rose into the night air. You could hear live music, the clang of an electric guitar; a man in a sombrero sang into the microphone.

I said, "Is that Portuguese?"

Mother listened for a second. "I'm very good on my romance languages, except for Portuguese. I can never quite tell where one word ends and another begins."

"We had a Portuguese maid once," Gloria Styles said, "but she didn't shave under her arms. I told her that's not how we do things in Canada."

"Once they're gone, they're gone," Dr. Frum said, holding me by the sleeve with an imploring two fingers. Then I saw Claire English. Childlike features, short hair with curls wisping by her ears, exactly like in her obituary. She was talking to a group of stylish women in their thirties. For a second I thought of ignoring her, of not being too easily available. She'd never liked that about me. *But surely this is not the time for that.* She caught sight of me and cocked her head with a sort of sad affection.

"I owe you such an apology," she said.

"It was a long time ago," I said.

"I used to watch you on television and I'd think, Does he ever think about me?"

"I think about you all the time."

"But you think about everything all the time. That was part of your charm." She put her hand on my arm. "But that's not really what you want to talk about, is it? You're just being polite."

I said, "I'm looking for someone." My voice wobbled. "But I think I'll kill myself if he's here."

She whispered in a friend's ear, who shot me an alarmed look. They spoke together for another moment and then Claire, with an entirely different rhythm, said, "You better come with me."

When we emerged from the tunnel, we were on the other side of a canal. The city twinkled behind us.

"We were lucky to get a taxi," Claire said. "It's fiesta this week." I said nothing.

The car turned inland; the smell of the sea retreated. Houses with brightly lit exteriors, oranges and pinks and turquoises, grew farther and farther apart, until the jungle crowded both sides of the road, the moon standing round and unblinking over the treetops. Stones crackled and fired under the taxi; a cat disappeared into the foliage. The driver killed the engine, the headlights went out, we rolled to a stop. Up the road, half hidden in the jungle, was a yellow clapboard cottage. Suddenly you could hear the night noise from the jungle, crickets, frogs, moist things. We sat silently. A black child appeared on the stairs of the yellow cottage, pausing on the porch and then going in.

I said, "Is that it?"

"That's it," she said.

I got out of the car.

"Do you want me to wait?"

I didn't answer. I left the door open (I didn't want a slam to alert the people in the house) and ran softly up the road until I was just outside the circle of light in front of the house. A soft orange poured from the curtained windows. I went up on the porch. A glass mobile tinkled overhead. A sound like broken glass. I put my hand on the doorknob. I listened. A television was playing inside. A live soccer game; you could hear the human swell in the background.

I turned the knob and went in.

A little boy with sleepy eyes turned away from the television set toward me. I covered the length of the room in a few steps, I swept him into my arms, I burst into tears, I could smell him, feel him. I said, "Just stay like this. Just for a second."

I held him. I thought, I'll count to ten and if he's not gone by ten, then he's real. He's real and I'm here.

I said, "Simon, I can't stand to be away from you."

It took him a moment to understand what I was saying. He drew back his head so he could see all of my face, looking from one eye to the other. "You don't have to do that, Daddy."

"I *do*."

"No, you don't."

"No?"

"You'll be here anyway."

I said, "But I want to be here *now*."

He looked at me for a second. "Daddy, I'm all right."

I said, "You're so brave. How could you be so brave? You're all by yourself."

He shook his head. "I'm never by myself."

I kissed the top of his head. His blond hair thick and healthy and clean. "You'll wait for me?"

"Yes."

"You won't be sad?"

"Nope."

"Promise?"

"Yes." He put his small fingers on my face. "Don't be sad, Daddy." He wiped the tears from my eyes. "Don't be sad," he said.

3

I went back to work. I put on my makeup, I went to the set, I interviewed my guests, then I went back to my dressing room. Jessica came by, told me how good I was doing. Then I took off my makeup, got my briefing notes for the next day's show. And went back home.

People were gentle with me. The makeup girl stopped asking if Tom Cruise was gay, the soundman didn't make any jokes about how much money on-air guys must get. So I did my job. I never went beyond the script, though, never beyond the ten neatly typed questions Jessica put in my hand each morning. A woman who made bridges out of spaghetti, an Israeli politician with a chip on his shoulder, a television actor who'd just made his first feature film, it didn't matter. I asked my ten questions and then I said goodbye.

Initially, I'd thought that being back on television, just the risk of doing poorly, of looking bad, might suck my attention from my wound, might make me think about something else for a while. But it didn't. It didn't work at all.

What did work, and I didn't reflect on it for some time, was an episode that happened to me one night when I was out walking. It was past midnight, a clear night, stars very distinct in the sky; you could feel the cold air sizzle in your lungs. I was walking along Davenport, a treeless, industrial strip, the kind of neighbourhood that puts a steel hand on your heart. On the south side, down a bit from nothing, is a lumberyard, and I noticed that in the back of the lot there was a tiny shack with a light in it. I don't know why but I jumped the chain-link fence and started across the parking lot toward the shack. A Doberman pinscher, a big, sleek one, appeared in front of me without a sound. Not a growl, nothing. He just stood there, those black button eyes, those cut-off ears pressed against his head, staring; an animal capable of tearing out your throat without changing his expression. I started to back up. I didn't take my eyes off him, one step, two steps, edging across the parking lot until my back was pressed to the fence. Then he came closer, close enough to touch; still not a sound. I didn't turn around, I knew if I tried to climb the fence he'd attack. So I stood where I was, not looking at him, motionless.

The doorway lit up in the little shack and a shaggy man ambled out. Didn't call out or run. Just walked over until he stood behind the dog.

"Can I help you?" he said.

"I'm looking for my son."

"Step into the light there." I did as he asked. Then he said, "You're the guy who went to the bar."

"That's right."

"Well, he's not here."

I said, "Can you open the fence for me?"

"Can't."

"Why not?"

"It's padlocked from the outside."

I said, "I'll have to go over the top then."

He said, "That's how you came in."

"The dog's not going to be a problem?"

"No, he's fine. Don't worry about *him*." It sounded like a private joke between the two of them.

I started over the fence, my arms shaking, the links rattling. He made no offer of assistance. When I hopped down, I rubbed my hands together; they were burning. "Well," I said, "thanks a lot."

"Doesn't take long, does it?" he said. "You turn your back, blam, she's gone."

It was only when I was back on the freezing street that I realized that for a few minutes there, when the dog first appeared, when it looked as if he would strike, I had thought about something other than Simon. "Are you still there?" I whispered, my breath in clouds. Yes, he was.

"Did you think I'd gone away?"

My boss called me into his office, asked me how it was going. I said fine. Did I come back too soon? No, not too soon. Was I seeing someone, getting some help? I said no, I didn't need help, I needed my son back. He gave me a rather grand speech; he meant well, I suppose, it just wasn't the time to be quoting *Henry V*.

Later that afternoon, I stopped by Jessica Zippin's desk. I was looking for a fine-point pen, she always had a stack of them. She wasn't there, was in an editing suite probably, but she'd left the weekly ratings on her desk. It was a noontime current-affairs show, pretty light stuff, very popular with gays and waiters. You could get a table anywhere in town.

For the first few days after I was back, the ratings were terrific, nearly a million people, which was about twice what we usually got. The curiosity factor, I guess. Talk-show host loses child; let's have a look. But then things started to fall off.

I should have quit, perhaps, but the truth is I didn't know what to do all day without a job, what I'd do in the morning or the afternoon or the evening or the day after or the month after or the years after. It was numbing to think about all that time.

Jessica came into the makeup room one morning. There was a mistake in the script, she said. Here, it should be Ralph Klein, not *Calvin* Klein. He was the clothes guy. And while I was talking, explaining that I knew all that, I saw that she was looking at my lips, and I had a feeling, a very strange one indeed, that she wanted to kiss me, that my being so sad about my son kind of turned her on. Maybe I'm being cruel. Maybe she just wanted to save me.

"My mother's a big fan of yours," she said.

"Uh-huh."

"She watches you slavishly."

"That's nice."

"She asked me to ask you if you were Jewish."

"No, I'm not Jewish."

"That's what I said. But she said you've got to be a bit Jewish to talk the way you do."

"No, I'm not Jewish."

"Anyway, she asked me if she could meet you some-time. That'd really give her a thrill."

"That's very flattering."

"Maybe you could come out to dinner with us."

I saw that she was being kind. "Dinner with you and your mom?"

"Well, there'd be another guy there too."

"Oh."

"She's got a new husband. He's a real asshole but they go everywhere together."

"That's too bad."

"What is?"

"Having an asshole for a stepfather."

"Please, he's not my stepfather. He's just an asshole." She paused. "She wants me to give back my house key."

"Really?"

"She told me he doesn't like the kids just dropping around whenever they feel like it. Letting themselves in."

I said, "So she asked for the key back."

"Right."

"Jesus," I said.

"She's done it before."

The makeup girl was waiting. I said, "Done what before?"

"She married this Czechoslovakian guy. Moved him into the house just like that. I didn't come out of my room for three years."

"Nothing inappropriate, I hope."

"No, just a creep. Just a creep living in my house." She wiped, I thought, a few tears from her cheek. "I told her, I said, 'I'll throw away the key, Mom, but I'm not going to give it back.'"

The floor director came in. He saw the makeup girl applying mascara to her own eyes in the mirror, Jessica in tears. "Wheels up in five minutes," he said and got out of there.

"I'll tell you what," I said, "I'll come to dinner with you and your mom. This guy too. I'll tell him how fantastic you are."

"He won't listen."

"I'll tell him how fantastic you are and if he doesn't respond in the right spirit, I'll fix him."

"As in fix his wagon?"

"Exactly."

"He's got big ears," she said. "Really big ears. Like cabbages."

It had been about six weeks now, the snow mostly gone, running in the sewers; you could hear it first thing in the morning, this water running and wet car tires on pavement. Some mornings when I looked out the window and saw it was another grey day I thought God was doing it to me on purpose, making it as bad as possible, so that when Simon came home, it'd be all the better. The sun'd come out, water would stop running in the gutters. The peculiar thing is, Simon adored the rain. He was the only kid I ever met who did. He'd sit by the window, his little breath fogging the glass, and watch it come down. Once I asked him, I said, "What are you watching out there, Simon?" But he didn't answer, he just stared and stared, like he was watching a movie. It was as if the rain made the movie in his little brain all the more vivid. I don't know. It was hard to get his attention when he was sitting by the window and it was raining.

The police called every three or four days but they didn't come by anymore. There was a new missing child in the newspaper. A new favourite. It's terrible but he seemed like the competition. His parents were split up; the father had taken him on a trip to the Caribbean and not come back. The mother was distraught. She went on television. Gave too many interviews. It looked as if she made herself up for the camera. I remember watching her and thinking they were assholes, not working it out together, the mother and the father. At least they still had him, at least they knew where he was.

I went out that night. I stood in the middle of the street, and then I headed north. I walked and walked and walked but I couldn't feel anything. I ended up in front of my old house in Forest Hill. Looking back up at my old bedroom. What was I doing there? Following an old route, an old rut. Across the street, where dead Johnny Best used to live, the door opened; a gold bar of light spilled onto the front walk. A woman stood there, staring. I turned my back to her. Then heard her footsteps, clack, clack, clack on the sidewalk.

"Can I help you?" she said.

"I used to live here."

"Somebody else lives there now."

"I imagine they do."

"Well, they're not here now. They're in Ireland. Are they expecting you?"

"No."

"When I saw you standing here, I thought maybe you were a robber."

"No, I'm not a robber."

"If you stand out here like that, looking at the house, people'll think you're a robber. That you're casing the place."

"I just came back for a look."

"It's a strange night for a trip down memory alley," she said, less sure of herself now.

"There you go."

"Do I know you?" she said.

"No."

"You look familiar."

I said, "Did you know that the boy who used to live in your house cut his throat with a straight razor?"

That shut her up.

I went on. "He wanted to be a concert pianist. He used to practise so hard his mother had to clean the blood off the keys in the morning."

She went very still. "How do you know that?"

"Like I said, I used to live there. You see that bedroom right there? That was my mother's. She's dead now too."

"I'm going in," the woman said. "I wouldn't stay out here too long. People'll wonder what you're up to. They might even phone the police."

I heard her clack, clack, clack on the walkway leading to her house; then the door opened and shut. I knew she was watching me, that if I turned my head I'd see her small face in the window. But I didn't look. It seemed like an admission of guilt. I just stayed long enough not to be pushed around and then left.

What if I *had* been robbing the house? What would it be like to steal through those old rooms, the air dark like velvet, knowing my way around? The foyer, the seventeen stairs to the second floor; my old bedroom across the hall, the bathroom, my mother's room where nightly she lay on a stack of white pillows, watching television and smoking cigarettes. Her door open. *Oh, Roman, it's you.*

I took a taxi up to the family cemetery. It was closed up but I hopped over the spiked iron fence. I'd never been there before at night. Snow lay in melting drabs over the gravestones; you could hear water running there too. A light burning in the stone cottage at the edge of the property. I followed a slow, scythe-shaped path into the heart of the graveyard. It was a damp night, clouds hurrying by the moon like angry aunts. Stone monuments rising on my left, little headstones, a large cross; I went on another hundred yards and there it was, the family plot, the names of dead uncles and my poor sister and my father and mother, all etched in the black marble. My mother, dead twenty years now. Dead longer in my life than she had been alive in it. Yet how immediate she seemed, so vivid. That red scarf around her neck, dancing in the living room with a black man; the windows thrown open, the salt air blowing in from the sea. She was quite the dancer and knew it. You could hear that music too, foolish, dirty lyrics, the bend-down-low verses she so adored. *Roman, Roman, join us, join us, no one's watching.* Her slacks rolled up like clam diggers, her shirt tied at her waist. *You'll never learn to dance if you don't learn to stop being so damn self-conscious.* Dancing on the carpet with the black man in blue pants.

I said to the slab of black marble, "Mother, I have to get back there." The calypso music stopped.

"Just go to sleep, dear. That's how you used to make Santa Claus come."

"It's not working. You have to help me."

She was dancing again, the black man smiling, watching her.

"Your mother dances better than my wife," he said.

I said, "Tell me how to get back there, Mother. Tell me. Do this one thing for me. I'll never ask you for anything more."

"Just go to sleep," she said. "It's simple. Go to sleep. And leave the window open. You always dream better when the window is open."

When I hopped back over the iron fence, I saw a pair of headlights go on at the far end of the street. I didn't move; I knew they would come this way, that they would stop.

"How are you doing?" he said. It was the cop with the greasy hair. And it suddenly occurred to me that I'd spotted his car (its rundown, tiresome lines) earlier in the night when I left my apartment, and then again when I crossed the street to the cemetery.

I said, "You're following me."

"Not really."

"You are."

He sighed. "We just want to make sure a difficult situation doesn't get worse."

"Meaning what?"

"Get in. I'll run you home."

I went around the side of the car, got in, a tabloid newspaper between us. We pulled away slowly, the blinker clicking. No one else on the road; the asphalt gleaming here and there in patches.

I said, "Do you think you need your blinker this time of night?"

"The law's the law," he said. Was he apologizing or was he joking? The sound of water under the wheels. The car smelt like a small town. A taxi went by in the other direction, the dark-skinned driver looking over at us and then quickly away. We turned right on St. Clair, headed over to Spadina, down through that yawning park, across the bridge, around Casa Loma and down into Chinatown.

He pulled to a stop in front of my house. Put on the emergency brake and turned to face me. But didn't say anything.

I said, "Can I get out now?"

"There's something about you, Roman. I can't quite put my finger on it. But I will."

"Put your finger on what?"

"You break into a man's house. You break into a cemetery—"

"I didn't break into a cemetery."

"How did you get in?"

"You know how I got in."

"That's breaking and entering. I could run you in for that."

"Why don't you?"

He chuckled. "I'm not afraid of the newspapers, Roman. If I were, I could never do my job."

"So. Are you going to run me in?"

He took a moment to stare up the street, almost as if he saw something down there, near the bar; then, releasing his attention, he turned back to me. "Where are you keeping him, Roman?"

I went to see Dr. Marvin Rickman. He was a slim, good-looking man. You couldn't tell his age, maybe fifty, maybe sixty. He was a show-biz doctor; you never knew who you'd see in the waiting room. Randy Quaid, maybe, Christopher Plummer, Brian Dennehy, Susan Sarandon, all those folks shooting movies in town, waiting to go down the hall with their file in their hands. Okay, Miss Sarandon, away you go. You'd hear her say, "Hey, Marv," cheerful, engaged voice; then Marv, cool, not in a sweat having stars around, "Hey, Susan." Then the door shut. It was only the goofs who made him come by the set, people who thought they were going to get mobbed in the waiting room. Them he charged a thousand dollars a crack, didn't matter what the visit was, a vitamin B shot in the ass, a sore throat, an actor too high to remember his lines.

I said, once the door was shut, "I've got to get some pills, Marv."

He said, "How's it going?" Not looking up from my file. Writing something down. He was like a judge that way. Always writing. But always listening, too.

I said, "I can't stand the pain. It's peeling me right down to the bone."

"The police making any progress?"

I said, "They interviewed an old girlfriend of mine."

"Oh yeah?"

"I ran into her down at the police station. She had sweat stains under her arms. They must have really grilled her."

He kept writing. I said, "They're talking to people who come to the house sometimes. M.'s friends. That kind of thing. It wasn't one of them. I know it."

He nodded sympathetically. Asked how M. was. Not good. How were we? Okay, I said. Under the circumstances. I brought the subject back to the pills.

He looked up. "I'm not sure this is a good idea."

I said, "Marv, this is not recreational." He smiled privately, just so I could see it. He was a very hip guy; that's why all the movie stars liked him.

"Take one of these when things get bad," he said, and opened his drawer and gave me a sample pack. Twelve caplets.

I said, "They're always bad, Marv. Can't you give me something that'll last?"

He ignored that. "But be careful, they've got a rebound effect. You feel better for the moment—the next day, it's even worse."

I took all the pills that day; I swear they couldn't have lasted more than a few minutes each. I called him back the next day and asked for something else, something with purchase.

There was a silence. Then he said, "You must have known what the answer would be before you even called."

He gave me the name of a psychiatrist friend of his. He said, "Do you have a pen?"

I didn't but I said sure.

He spelled out the name and the phone number and I pretended to write it down and then hung up.

It was the strangest thing: when I was trying to get the pills, I had a feeling of being disloyal to Simon. Like cheating on an exam.

4

I slept badly that night. The couch felt bumpy and I was hot. But then, just before daylight, when I had given up hope, I fell asleep and returned effortlessly to the Caribbean town. Still nighttime. I was sitting on a park bench. In the distance, a couple of streets over, you could hear the fiesta raging, the man in the sombrero hollering, some kind of singalong. He did a verse; the crowd did a verse. I saw a group of children appear at the mouth of a street opposite the park. They were laughing and bumping into each other; they'd come down the wrong street and now had to turn around. I saw Simon with them. He was talking to a little girl, their heads very close together. I thought, He's with his friends, I'll let him come over when he's ready. But when he saw me, the smile fell from his face. I was up and out of my seat in a second. He had started back up the street when I caught up to him.

"Simon," I said, "don't cut me off. Please."

He turned and beamed. "I didn't see you."

"You didn't?"

"I was talking to my friend."

I said, "I was afraid you were mad at me."

He shook his head. "Uh-uh."

I said, "I've made such a hash of things, Simon. But I love you so much. Can I stay here a little bit? Just be with you? I am so hungry for you."

He looked up the street at the retreating children. You could see he wanted to be with them but he didn't want to hurt my feelings.

"You can go with them," I said.

"Yes?"

"Yes. Absolutely. Go with your friends. I just needed to see you. I was afraid that you'd cut me off."

"No, Daddy."

"Just promise me that you'll never cut me off and then I'll be happy."

"I'll never cut you off."

"Then go," I said, giving his small shoulder a nudge. "Go play with your friends. I'll be around."

"You're sure?"

"As sure as sure."

I kissed him on the top of his head, inhaling the smell of that thick hair. His hair. The way his room smelt. And then I watched him run up the street in his brown shorts and his red sandals. He was never very athletic, Simon. He had a way of running that broke my heart, as if he were charging at something, as if the excitement of life was more than his limbs could balance.

"You have to move out," M. said. She was standing at the foot of the couch. For a second I thought she had a knife in her hand, that she was going to stab me to death.

"You have to move out," she said. "I can't stand the smell of you in the apartment."

I moved into the Chelsea Hotel, a suite on the eighteenth floor. The network had a corporate deal with them. I could stay as long as I liked. As long as I worked with the show.

I called M. when I got there. I said, "I just wanted you to have my number."

"Why would I want your number?"

I said, "Sometimes I wish I could get hit by a car, or electrocuted, that something bad would happen to me—"

"Roman, I'm never, ever going to feel sorry for you."

I started to say something else but she cut that off too. "Please don't call. It's too disappointing to pick up the phone and have it be you."

In the late afternoons I lay on my bed up there on the eighteenth floor and stared out the window. Clouds drifted by. Sometimes it looked like the sky was broken and the clouds were showing through; sometimes it was the other way around. It was like being in an arcade. The clouds disappeared at the side of the window, you had the feeling they doubled back around on the other side of the sky and then replayed themselves. I waited for the beginning of the loop, the part I'd already seen. I said to myself, Is that it? Or is *that* it?

There was a knock on my door. It was a catamaran salesman from Daytona Beach on the wrong floor. I heard his footsteps moving away down the hall and then I went back to watching the clouds crawl across the sky.

Sometimes I fantasized about the phone ringing. It's the police, they've found him. I imagined running to the station; there he was, at the end of the corridor, holding on to a detective's hand. I'd sweep him up in my arms. No, I'd drop to my knees and hug him on that level. I'd call his mother. I'd say, I know you told me not to call——.

Thinking about all this, I could feel the chemistry in my body changing.

Sometimes I'd imagine the other call. I'd peer down into a tiny coffin and I'd say, "I'm sorry, but that's not him." Which is to say that I'd be sorry for some other parent, the gangly Englishman who had followed me into the police station.

Then for the thousandth time, I'd run through the events of the evening I lost him. I imagined the telephone ringing just as I headed down the street. Of course, I'd answer it. It'd take only minutes, maybe longer, but that thing, that black spirit that moves around the world, that thing that scooped him from my porch, would have passed by. I've always thought evil was like that: if you can only not be there when it brushes by.

I talked to Simon constantly. About my day, my childhood, my parents. I talked to him about what I was doing even while I was doing it. *There's more flavour when you scramble eggs slowly, Simon. Don't ask me why.* I believed he was listening to me. I wanted him to think well of me, be amused by me. Interested by me. Comforted by me. I believed in my heart that he forgave me.

Nighttime I floated through the city. I found myself gravitating toward underground clubs. I liked the basements, the candles on the tables, the jazz trio in the shadows. I liked the garish amateur murals on the wall, a bird with three heads. I drank house merlots that tasted like blood. I sat with my back to the wall, the music bubbling like a pudding or a thick soup.

The waiters I knew by name. I tipped them well. Sometimes I fell asleep in my chair and one of them, very gently, almost like a mother, tugged at my sleeve. "Roman," they said. "Roman, *are you inside there?*"

Sometimes the musicians came over on their break. They introduced themselves, they introduced their girlfriends.

"Please," I said and indicated a chair. They thought I could do something for them. Everyone did.

They slipped me their CDs or the galleys of their novels. They seemed to think I gave a shit about the upward trajectory of their careers. Did I know their movie had been invited to the Tehran Film Festival? Could they send me a tape? The novels were the worst, always the same shit, good-hearted cretins overcoming adversity and emerging as finer human beings. One night I took a rosy-cheeked kid aside (it was his first novel) and said, "For a guy who takes it up the ass seven ways to Thursday, your character sure shows some spunk."

"Right," he said hopefully, if a bit guardedly.

"Of course, in my experience, people tend to get worse as they get older, not better."

You could see the disappointment on his face. He must have thought I was a different kind of person. You watch someone on television, after a while you figure you know them.

"Really?" he said.

"And then some."

But I accepted their movies and their novels and their CDs and their theatre posters with good grace. I congratulated them for "sticking with it," and then I dumped the whole works down the garbage chute back at the hotel.

Not one of them ever asked about Simon or anything else. Why is that?

One evening a kid in a white shirt dedicated a song to me; a small spotlight found me. I shielded my eyes and gave a small bow. There was a pleasant ripple of applause. Like rain on the roof when you're little. I sat back down; the evening proceeded forward. *Please, you're too kind. Really.*

I remember a waitress leading me gently to a waiting taxi that night. "See you soon," she said and gave me a kiss on the cheek. I could feel where she'd kissed me.

I said to the driver, "Just drive, please."

He said, "Where?"

I said, "I don't care."

He said, "You must want to go somewhere."

I said, "Don't get me started." He put his arm up on the seat back and turned around to get a good look at me.

I said, "I just love being in a car at night."

We pulled away. "Do you mind if I play some music?" he said into the rear-view mirror.

"Help yourself. Just nothing too strident." I leaned back and closed my eyes, the music playing in the dark car, the driver moving us quietly through the streets. I was quite drunk, and somewhere down by the lakeshore, the black water on my left, I conked out and dreamt about going back to the little Caribbean town. The fiesta was in full swing, but there was no sign of Simon, no sign of my mother among the party-goers. The man in the sombrero, wearing a fresh red shirt, was calling out names from the bandstand. He'd call out a name, there'd be a huge cheer, then he called out another one. It was a list of the recently deceased.

I caught sight of the handsome young man in the military jacket. He was short with perfect features, dark thick hair. I remembered now where I knew him from.

I said, "I saw you the other night." He nodded. After a moment I went on, "Forgive me for saying it, but it was so sad when you died."

"It took rather a long time, didn't it?" he said pleasantly.

"It's the greatest death in literature."

"So I've been told," he said.

"Do people tell you that?"

"All the time," he said. "You can't imagine the things people say to me."

The orchestra swung into "J'attendrai."

I said, "I have a favour to ask you."

"Oh yes?" he said, showing his small perfect teeth. You could see he was used to people asking him favours.

"Prince! Prince!" a middle-aged woman called from the crowd. "You promised me. You did. You absolutely *promised* me."

"Would you excuse me?" he said.

"Please, first my favour. It's very small. Prince, please." He paused diplomatically. I said, "I need to get someone out of town."

"It's fiesta," he said. "There are no taxis, even for the ailing."

I said, "I thought maybe you might know someone——"

He put a small hand on my shoulder. "If you're not dead," he said, "I can't help you."

I spotted my mother coming down a narrow lane holding a small boy by the hand.

5

It was spring now, you could smell the freshly turned earth, and on one of those evenings, I directed the cab to an address in my old neighbourhood. It's a lamp store now but it used to be a coffee house. I went there with M. the first night we slept together. An ancient black blues singer was playing that night, I remember, plunking and humming and going unnoticed on the stage. A university crowd, who had campaigned only that afternoon for daycare rights, talked all the way through his set.

Why did I go there on that particular night? I was driving myself ragged following every whisper of an impulse. *Perhaps this is the place, perhaps at the end of that street; if I count to ten before crossing at the light, perhaps I'll end up behind the car in which I will see his face in the rear window.*

As my taxi pulled up to the lamp store, I saw a silhouette sitting with her chin in her hand on the front stoop. A clutch of enamel shapes gleaming in the window behind her. For a second I wondered if I was hallucinating. She didn't move, didn't seem surprised to see me when I got out of the cab. As if I'd just stepped out of her head.

"Do you want me to sit down?" I said.

She took her chin out of her hand. "Not particularly."

I tried to put my hands in my pockets but they wouldn't go all the way in.

"We had him to look forward to, Roman," M. said. She was nodding her head, as if she was agreeing with something. "We had him to look forward to *all that time*."

The cab driver rolled down his window and lit a cigarette. He reminded me of a dog eating from a dish, looking around while he's chewing, nothing registering.

She said, "I'm trying to think, again, why you didn't go in the bar, look around, go, 'Yeah, that's great but I shouldn't be here,' and then go back home."

I could feel my arms crossing involuntarily over my chest.

"Why *did* you stay?" she said.

I didn't say anything.

"If you'd had a pot on the stove, you would have gone home."

I said, "Do you want to take my cab? I'm happy to walk."

"You're happy?"

"I said I'm happy to *walk*."

She was nodding again. "I must have been pretty arrogant back then, Roman?"

"When?" I said.

"When I met you."

"How's that?"

Carefully, as if she were speaking to a dim-wit. "Because I believed back then that no one could wreck my life." Pause. "It's like that story, you know, the one about the guy, what's his name?"

"Humpty Dumpty."

"Right. Humpty *Dumpty*." There was a patch of hair missing from the side of her head, about the size of a silver dollar. I could see it under the street light. It had fallen out the day she heard about our son and had never grown back.

"Just keep moving, Roman. Keep going."

It was a long weekend, and just thinking about all that empty, unstructured time put me into a panic. I hurried downstairs and talked to the concierge in the lobby. He was from Atlanta, he liked it up here, liked the city. "That's the trouble with Atlanta," he said. "It has no centre of gravity." We talked about places with no centre of gravity. I told him about a park I used to live beside when I was in university. Everyone loved it. But it depressed me. It didn't seem to matter what angle you came into the park at, you never felt you were at its centre. We both agreed that Queen's Park, north of the parliament buildings, had a centre. "The statue," he said.

I finished the sentence for him. "The man on the horse."

"That's why everyone sits near there," he said. "That's the centre. People can feel it."

I went outside. The sunlight had that peculiar overly bright quality you feel on the first morning of a Caribbean vacation. A couple stopped me on the street, told me how much they liked the show, could I do a piece sometime on their aunt, she collected jam jars. I said sure. When I got up to Yorkville, the place was uncharacteristically empty. Where was everyone? They couldn't all have summer cottages, be out on the porch airing out mattresses and listening to music with the volume turned up, the lake sparkling just over their shoulder. I had a coffee at an outdoor café. A couple with matching yawns walked by. I talked to the waiter for a while. It was a friendly enough world; there just didn't seem to be anyone in it. A tall kid on a bicycle rode slowly down the street; you could tell he was killing time, too. Waiting for Monday morning. No, worse, Tuesday morning. I forgot. There was another day of this. I looked at my watch. It seemed to have stopped; maybe it was slow. I looked at the second hand. It was moving. But how could only fifteen minutes have lapsed? It seemed so much longer. I thought maybe I'd look up a friend and then I realized I didn't have any. I could look up Howard Glass. But I couldn't forgive him the private pleasure he took in my misfortune. The hand-rubbing self-congratulation that this had happened to me and not to him.

Other people? Let me put it this way. Before I got on television I thought people weren't interested in me because I hadn't accomplished enough in my life. But after I got on television, nothing changed. I didn't have fewer friends but I didn't have more either, and for a while I assumed it was because I was now too accomplished, had done too much, had had too many interesting conversations with too many interesting people to be bothered with them. But then I realized, and it didn't take very long, that that wasn't it either. That the people who didn't want to have anything to do with me didn't want to have anything to do with me, no matter what I did or didn't do. Just because I was me and they were them, if you follow. Which, in a way, was sort of a liberation, however lonely at times. And the truth is, after a certain while, a certain age, it's too much trouble to make new friends, all that chat, the dinners, the excitement, the laughter, the old jokes trotted out all over again. Too much work. It was like that evening that Jessica Zippin had proposed, with her mother and the new husband. Just the thought of it, the getting dressed, walking to the restaurant, the chirpy chit-chat, the threadbare celebrity anecdote (maybe the one about Robert Redford, that still had some material on the sleeves), the evening winding down with coffee and comfortable chuckles, the shaking of hands in front of the restaurant, the promise to do it again soon, the smile dropping from the maître d's face the second his back was turned, God, it just seemed fucking intolerable.

I looked around the café. This wasn't a whole lot better, either. There must be a place, I thought, some small place where I'm not pinched. A temporary reprieve, I mean, from the here and now. But where would it be? Then I realized, for the four-millionth time, like a man who keeps counting and recounting his money, hoping it'll come to a better total, that I'd never be happy again until I found Simon. That I would carry the sensation in my body like a toothache forever. And if he was dead? Well, he wasn't. It was that simple. I couldn't imagine where he was, I couldn't imagine how anyone could conceal a six-year-old boy, the newspapers and the television buzzing with his picture (at least for a while). But they had. Someone had him. Somewhere. Someone who wanted him. So there was nothing to be done but find him. Go back to looking. Get up right now and go somewhere.

But I didn't. I couldn't get up out of my seat. I thought about going north or east but it all seemed the same to me. I said, "You'll have to speak up, Simon."

The waiter, who was taking tall beer glasses off the next table, said, "I'm sorry?"

I paid the bill, made a joke about something and headed uptown. I thought I'd walk up Yonge Street, maybe something'll pull me this way or that—

Bear with me a little longer. Just a bit.

I walked till nightfall and then I went into a movie. I thought, Pick a movie that won't make you more upset. I looked at all six of them on the marquee, then realized they would all upset me, either too jarring or too sad or accusatory somehow in their blandness, so I went to the one that was just starting. The theatre was pretty full, which was comforting, and I sat near the back on the aisle so I could make a quick escape. Nearly a quarter of the way in, during a quiet part, I was aware of a couple sitting near the front, a bald young man and a girl. It was a date or something, and he was talking to her, but talking as if they were alone in their living room, watching television. I was just about to get up and find an usher (he looked on the tough side, that bald head) when someone shouted, "Shut up!"

There was a ripple of laughter. But the laughter stopped when the man leapt to his feet and looked around. "Who the fuck said that!"

He scrutinized the theatre; the place went dead still. Five hundred people terrified he was going to pick them. He pushed his way to the edge of the row and started up the aisle, looking this way and that, the movie playing, everyone pretending to pay attention. "Who said it? Who told me to shut up?"

When he got to me, when he was about five feet away, I put up my hand. I put up my hand and I said, in a voice not entirely my own, "I did." And in the steps that he took toward me, fast, bang, bang, bang, I felt free of my horror. I thought, It doesn't matter what comes of this, it's better than before.

He said, "Did you say that?" But there was a hint of uncertainty in his voice. He was a bully, and the notion that a fair fight might be coming his way frightened him. Enraged him, too. For a hushed audience watched him. He had to do something.

I said, "Yes." And looked at him. I thought, This is it, This is the sensation I've hungered for. But he didn't move. It was as if something dark had strode through his imagination.

"Fuck!" he shouted. Then he shouted it again. It was like watching an animal throw itself against the bars of its cage. But it was slipping away from him, he needed more, and I knew not to give it to him. Suddenly there was a hole where he'd been standing and then a hole where the usher had been standing. His girlfriend followed him out, looking down, a dumb beast of a creature, and for the next few minutes, while the adrenalin settled back down, I was happy. I'll admit it. I thought, So that's the way to go.

A few days later, a guy I vaguely knew from the sports department, Peter somebody, told me that he was shopping for a new house. A bunch had just come on the market that morning, his wife was out of town, did I want to go with him, have a look? It was such a naked invitation I said yes. I wasn't sure why he invited me, maybe he felt sorry for me, but I didn't want him to regret a generous impulse.

So later that afternoon a blue Toyota picked us up in front of the studio. The real estate agent had a small, pointed face, like a muskrat, and she smelt as if she was on a diet. She didn't seem too happy to see my friend had brought someone along. Better to have him on his own, I suspect. Be the prevailing voice in the room.

We headed up into the Annex, pulled to a stop in front of a small brick house. Price half a million dollars. We went inside. It was gleaming clean but the sort of place a short man should live in. We went from room to room, stooping here and there, ending up in a living room with highly polished floors and an echo when you spoke. The agent was giving her routine, how the owners had put a lot of money into the place, how it had good bones, always think of the resale value, when she suddenly stopped.

"So what do you think?" she said. Smiling.

"Pretty close," my friend said, "but not quite there."

"What do you mean, not quite there?" she asked, pleasantly unpleasant.

"It just seems like a lot of money for a small place. Nice but small."

"You might think about readjusting your expectations, Peter," she said. *Peter.* That was the voice from the vice-principal's office.

"What about you?" she said, turning to me. "What do you think?"

"I like a place where you don't have to *wear* the bathroom," I said. She didn't find that funny at all. Peter did, but not her. I said, breaking the tension, "Do you know where the bathroom is, by the way?"

"I don't live here," she said.

I set off to find it myself. I wandered into the master bedroom. On the bedside table was a photograph, a father, mother and a son, Simon's age. The father was holding a paddle; so was the little boy; he looked like a miniature version of his father, trying to hold the paddle at exactly the same angle, except it was too big for him.

I went into the bathroom and sat down on the toilet. I could hear the agent going on about the finishings, the tile work. I looked around the room. A kid's painting on the wall, happy fish on the shower curtain; a medicine cabinet marked MEDICINE CABINET. That struck me as peculiar. Why would someone mark it? I got up and opened the cabinet door. A rusty hinge shrieked.

From outside I heard, "Roman, what are you doing in there?" He wanted me back out front. Didn't want to face that bitch alone. I said, "Just a second." I'm not in the habit of going through people's mail or personal stuff, but I had a sort of compulsion to snoop around inside the cabinet. As if there might be something important in there for me.

There was the usual stuff, creams, bath salts, dental floss, a stray tampon, a few hair pins, a hairbrush with blond hairs in it. I checked the pill bottles: headache stuff, pills for heartburn, cramps, bottles with names I didn't recognize. I was just about to close up when, hang on, what's this, right at the back there. A bottle of green pills. The print was very small. I stepped over to the window. Morphine tablets. Nearly a full bottle of them. Somebody must have had cancer in that house; you don't have stuff like that around otherwise. Tucking them out of sight, almost hidden, meant they knew it was serious but assumed the housing market wasn't crawling with drug addicts.

I felt a flush of pleasure. Anticipation, really. I thought, I bet that stuff works for everything. And just the sensation of having the bottle in my hand, the relief it would bring, made me feel better. I checked the date; only a week old. That wasn't good; that means they'd be missed. Still, if someone was really sick, they could get another script. Whereas me, well, just imagine going to

Marvin Rickman and saying, "I'm feeling a bit down today, Marv, I'd like some morphine tablets." He wasn't that hip.

"Hey, Roman, get out here."

"Coming, coming," I said. I closed the cabinet. Another shriek.

I stepped back into the hallway.

Peter said, "Listen, we're going to have a look at a couple of more houses. Do you want to come along?"

I said sure.

I didn't take one till bedtime. Then I poured myself a stiff belt of vodka, opened the pill bottle and shook a tablet into my hand. I stood naked at the window for a while, staring down at the city, Yonge Street going all the way north. The phone rang. It was Jessica Zippin; details about a show the following week. A crack-of-dawn interview with a lumber executive from Minneapolis. Only time we could get him. She said, "Write this down." I said, "Early morning shoot," and pretended to write it down, even repeating the date and time. It'd sort itself out, whatever it was.

Then the morphine came on; it came on in a warm, slow rush of reassurance. I ran a bath; I got in; I stared into the middle distance, just the splashing of the water, the sound of my bum against the porcelain. I took a deep breath. I thought, This wouldn't be a bad way to die. Not a bad way at all. Near midnight, I heffed myself out of the tub and flopped down on the bed. Didn't even cover myself up, just sailed away.

But the next day, it was a different story. I burst into tears on the way to work, I burst into tears in the make-up room. I did the show, everyone concerned because there was a sort of wobbly, rollercoaster feel to my questions. I may even have been a bit belligerent with a country-and-western singer. He was doing his regular-guy bit, how he loved his momma and stayed humble, when I observed, eyes at half-mast, that it was easy to stay humble when you sold fifty-five million albums. Jessica came on in my earpiece.

"He's our guest, Roman. Remember that. He's doing *us* the favour, not the other way around."

After the show, back in the makeup room, she popped her pretty face in the door, then came all the way in. She had a way of speaking, Jessica, of sighing and looking at the ceiling, as if she was thinking her way through something. It meant she had a complaint but didn't want a confrontation.

She said, "How'd the show go today?"

I said, "Fine," drinking down a glass of water. I was very thirsty and still a little rubber tongued from the morphine.

"You seemed a bit on edge," she said.

"This isn't an advertising agency, Jessica. Sometimes these guys should sing for their supper."

She said to the makeup girl, "Cindy, would you excuse us?"

Cindy left. Jessica shut the door. "You know, Roman, you're kind of the front man for the audience. You're supposed to ask the questions that they'd ask."

"Providing those are the right questions."

She laughed, but you could see she was trying to get somewhere. "You mean the audience is interested in the wrong stuff?"

"Sometimes, yeah, they're definitely interested in the wrong stuff."

"And you're going to straighten them out?" she said.

"Somebody should. Shit."

"Isn't that a bit like saying to a guy, your wife's not as pretty as you think?"

"I don't follow."

"Never mind. Bad example."

I said, "Am I in the doghouse here, Jessica?"

"No, no," she said. "You just seem in a funny mood today."

"Hey," I said, "remember that invitation you gave me, going out to dinner with you and your mom? I'd like to take you up on that."

6

It was a soft night, the sky streaked in blood, and I was thinking, Simon must be dead. He must be dead because you can't keep a six-year-old boy under wraps that long. I didn't really believe it, I think I was saying it to hurt myself. But then I thought, Fuck it, it doesn't matter because I'm going to be dead soon too and I'll see him in heaven, or I'll cease to exist altogether and there won't be a *me* to think about him anymore. Because for some time now, it had looked as if I was going to spend the rest of eternity missing him. It was almost a comforting idea, that you miss someone only as long as *you're* around.

I had read a story in the newspaper recently about an actor, a sort of pain-in-the-ass do-gooder who had lymphatic cancer zipping around his body like a pinball. When he got the prognosis (dead in three months) he claimed he'd hopped around the room, just bouncing with happiness. He'd had a full life, he said, it was time to leave the party. Besides which, he didn't want to oblige his friends to divert themselves from their lives to look after him. What a bullshitter, I thought, a liar right to the end. Can't come clean even now. I'd always suspected that under that modulated voice, that ostentatious public service, beat the heart of a manipulative prick.

I had been talking to Jessica about it that very morning. I was in the makeup chair and may have been a little emphatic in my condemnation because she did that thing she does, looked at the ceiling and sighed. I thought, What could she possibly be uncomfortable about? We barely knew the guy; I'd interviewed him years ago (no nukes), but then again, so had everyone in town: he saw to that.

I said, "What is it, Jessica?"

It turned out there was another part of the story that wasn't in the newspaper. About fifteen years ago, he bought his daughter a car for her birthday—she was nineteen—and about an hour after he gave her the keys and watched her go down the driveway a policeman came to the door and said she'd been killed in an accident.

He was watching television at the time and, when he heard the knock, he thought it was her, that maybe she'd come back for a second thank you. But it wasn't her and he never recovered; couldn't get away from the pain of it, not for even a day. And so when he got the news that he was dying of cancer, that he'd be dead soon, he really *did* hop up and down with joy, because it meant he wouldn't have to be sad about his daughter anymore.

It knocked the wind out of me, that story. I wondered if I'd ever got anything right. Like going down the street that winter night to see the girl band. Was it more than bad luck? Would it have been any better if I'd been going to the corner store? Would that make things more forgivable? Should I simply have never left the apartment for any reason? Was I alone in having done it? But, of course, it didn't matter now, did it? It was only the result that mattered. That's the thing that makes you know if you did right or wrong. But is that true? Always true? Doesn't matter. Doesn't matter, doesn't matter, doesn't matter.

And then I thought (going into the restaurant), I wonder if they'll let me switch places with Simon. I go to sleep down there; Simon wakes up here. Me, vanished without a sign. Without a trace. A few days' fuss, a few interviews with M.

But Simon, when he woke up back in the world, where exactly would he be? Where would he wake up?

So maybe I wasn't in an ideal mood to have dinner with Jessica and her family. They were already in the restaurant when I arrived, right at the back, near the wine rack, which ran the length of the wall.

A small man with white hair, wearing a smart blazer and an ascot, rose from his seat. "There you are," he said, shaking my hand. "My goodness, from all the things I've heard I half expected Johnny Carson to walk in the room."

Jessica was right. He did have big ears. David Lean had big ears too, but not like this guy. His stuck out.

Jessica's mother was still beautiful in her mid-sixties, perhaps a bit too much lipstick (probably his idea), but a lovely, narrow face, a generous bosom and intelligent eyes that looked directly into mine when she said, shaking my hand and bending close to me, "I'm terribly sorry." She said it gently and privately. Just between her and me. I'm not sure anyone else heard it. You could see her daughter had told her not to say anything but she'd decided that was wrong, this was something you acknowledged, however briefly. Jessica doodled on the paper tablecloth with a pen. From across the room, when I'd first caught sight of her, she had struck me,

I remember, like a sulky teenager having dinner with her parents. It was the guy, the new husband, Morley. She loathed him, and I had a feeling he loathed her back.

"Maybe you can resolve an argument for us," Morley said cheerfully. "I'm saying that TV reporters, people who do your job even at the highest levels, have someone prepare their questions for them." I looked at Jessica. She was still doodling.

"Sometimes they do, sometimes they don't," I said and winked at Mrs. Zippin. I winked because I wanted her to know that yes, her husband was an asshole, but no, I wasn't going to let it rile me. By the look on her face, a kind of expectation, I had the feeling that this sort of thing had happened before, that Morley was one of those guys who took pride in being "provocative."

"Take you, for example," he said, as if this was all great fun. "Do you write *your* questions?"

"Mostly."

"Really?"

"Yes."

"Then you must know a great deal. Tell me, how do you keep up?"

"Morley," his wife said, "this sounds like a cross-examination."

"Does it?" he said. "Does it, indeed?" Jessica stopped doodling for a moment and smiled privately to herself.

"I don't know how you do it," Mrs. Zippin said, "talking to those people like that. In front of a camera. I'm sure people could hear my heart beat all the way to Rochester."

"Who have you talked to?" Morley asked.

"Hundreds of people, actually. I've been doing this for a while."

"And the damn thing is, I've never seen you. Not once," he said.

"Well, it's a noonday show. Maybe you don't watch television during the day."

"Is that when it's on? I'm on the go all day. You're right. I just don't have the time for that stuff."

I waited a moment. "You know, Morley, people say that to me all the time. Sometimes they stop me on the street to tell me."

"Tell you what?" he said, friendly smile but alert, just at the edges.

"That they've never seen me on television before."

"Is that a fact?"

"And you know what else? It's almost invariably not true."

"Why do you suppose they say it, then?" he said, taking a sip of water. His mouth was drying, I could tell. So was mine.

I looked at Jessica, who was drawing a balloon but listening intently. "I think they tell me that, Morley, so I don't get too big for my britches."

The waiter appeared. Dressed *à la française*, white shirt, black pants, an apron. I ordered a martini. I normally don't drink gin but I had a feeling that tonight I was going to be able to drink a brace of them and feel nothing.

Two rather large women came into the restaurant; the maître d' knew them, they must have been regulars, and sat them beside the window. They pulled out their cell phones simultaneously as if they had been choreographed and laid them on the table. Afraid to miss that call. They gazed about the room, large, doughy faces and sharp eyes. Critical women.

"This is a lovely restaurant," Mrs. Zippin said. "I love going to new restaurants. We're quite adventurous that way. Do you know Chippin's? It's a new place over on Davenport. Very chic, indeed."

"The place with the really good-looking waiters?" Jessica asked.

"They couldn't be that good looking," Morley said in jolly tones, "or they wouldn't be just waiters."

"I don't know the place."

"Well, it's quite lovely," Mrs. Zippin said. "They keep the tables a proper distance apart. You don't feel like you're eating with the couple next door."

"You must have met quite a few movie stars in your time," Morley said. "Is it true they're short men with big heads?"

"Some of them."

"I saw you do that interview with Germaine Greer," Mrs. Zippin said. "She's a very clever woman but she shouldn't repeat herself like that."

"Like what, Mother?"

"She has an amusing routine, it's about how you can't rest your head in an Englishman's lap because they never dry clean their trousers." She paused. "No, you're right, it *is* amusing the first time. But when you hear it a second time, then it becomes something else. It becomes a ploy, almost, and the fun goes out of it entirely."

The waiter arrived. I took the martini and ordered an encore. Jessica looked at me with an amused frown.

"It's okay," I whispered, "I don't have a driver's licence."

"But you've got an interview tomorrow morning."

"Huh?"

"The lumber guy. You wrote it down."

"Can we order? If I don't eat by eight o'clock, I'm up half the night. You people eat so late here," Morley said, surveying the menu at arm's length. He fancied himself rather British, rather lordly the way he did it.

"We could," I said, feeling the first flush of the martini, "or we could drink some more."

Mrs. Zippin laughed.

"I understand you've had a recent sadness," Morley said, still looking at the menu and then up at me, over his reading glasses.

Jessica stopped doodling. Mrs. Zippin jerked her head toward him.

"I beg your pardon," I said.

"Oh," he said, as if surprised, "I wasn't to mention it."

When I got my breath back, I said, "Yes, I have."

"Dreadful," he said. "You're more of a man than I am. I can tell you that."

"How is that?" I said, my voice still shaky.

"Just getting through it."

"I'm not through it."

"No," he said, "I suppose one never really is." He waved the waiter over. "Dreadful," he said again, this time almost to himself, and returned his attention to the menu.

We ordered, I can't remember what, my appetite was gone, but slowly the conversation returned, slightly strained. I kept feeling that somehow I had been had, that there was a better answer than the one I'd given, something not so impotent. It was as if, while I was answering his question, I could feel my body shrinking, my clothes ill fitting, like I was a bum with dirty sleeves and food on my face. I kept thinking, I must have done something to deserve that. Could he have possibly intended so blatant a wound? People like Morley, I thought, looking at him across the table, he was eating his salad now, telling Jessica and her mother a clever story about living in South Africa, about running a bed and breakfast, how it was a lovely idea but simply too damn much work, people like Morley had a developed skill, they go right to the edge of things, they hover there. But if you call them on it, if you say, I know what you're doing and I don't like it, they shrug with bewilderment; they claim they don't have the foggiest idea what you're talking about. Even turn it back on you. Ask you why you're being so aggressive, so quick on the trigger.

He was getting to the punch line, you could see he'd told the story before, he was relishing the surefootedness of a successful party anecdote, the guaranteed pay-off, when I rose slowly to my feet, reached across the table and clapped him hard, as though popping a balloon, on both ears at the same time, and then when his hands went up to protect them, I joined my hands together and swung on him, catching him just under the chin. He flew off his chair. For a second I wondered if I'd killed him. The two large women froze in mid-chew; so did the couple at the next table. Even the waiter hesitated at the outer circle of the table.

What happened after that, the next few minutes, are a kind of electric smudge, although I'm not sure why. Perhaps there were traces of morphine still in my system. I'd tried taking half a tablet the night before to cut down on the chances of a rebound, but apparently to little effect. I hadn't had that much to drink, three martinis maybe, but I don't recall leaving the restaurant, except for the image of a grinning young man in a baseball cap. He was sitting near the door when they hustled me out, and I remember thinking he was an ally, the only person in the room who was on my side.

I needed help getting up the stairs to Jessica's apartment; I remember falling face forward in the guest room. Laughing, the whole thing a lark, a vindication; a prick that finally got his. I heard the door shut, no good night from Jessica, and then silence, as if she were wait-ing outside the door.

I returned, almost immediately, to the Caribbean town, this time walking up a street of soft lanterns like drooping flowers until I got to a cottage at the top. I lis-tened at the door, heard my mother talking, a one-way conversation, she must have been on the phone, and behind it, faintly, a television. I went in.

I said, "Is Simon here?"

"Just a second," she said into the phone and covered the mouthpiece. "He's in there, watching TV."

I must have hesitated or frowned because she said, "What?"

I said, "I hope he's not watching too much television."

"You watched television, dear, and look how you turned out."

"I mean he's not *just* watching television and noth-ing else."

"You should go in and see him now. He'll be sur-prised," she said.

"But he knew I was coming back?"

"Oh yes. He just didn't know when."

I knocked, a slight hesitant knock, and I went in. Simon was sitting on the floor with his plastic warriors and soldiers, little plastic men a finger length long.

"Hi," I said, whispering, as though it were late at night and I were coming home from a party. I kissed the top of his head. I didn't want to breathe alcohol on him.

"Daddy," he said.

"Listen, I want to talk to you about something. Can I turn the television off?" I sat on the floor beside him and took his small shoulders in my hands. "What do you think of this?" I said. "What if you and I switch places?"

"How do you mean?" he said.

"Look at me," I said. Then when he did, when he was still, I said, "Lord, your eyes are so beautiful I can barely stand it. But listen. What if I stay here and you go back to where I came from?"

The door opened. "Simon, do you still want those sandwiches?"

"Yes, please, Grandma."

"But I don't think we have any Coke," she said.

"You give him Coke?" I said.

"I gave you Coke."

"Doesn't it keep him awake all night?"

Simon put a small hand on my arm. "It's okay, Daddy. I have it every day."

"You do?"

"Yes, I do."

Mother went back out. He watched the door shut and kept his eyes there, dreaming. Awake but dreaming.

I said, "Simon?"

"Yes?"

"What do you think of my idea?"

"I can't do that, Daddy."

"Why not?"

"Because I live here now."

"With Grandma?"

"With *lots* of people," he said cheerfully.

"Simon," I said, "I'm so sorry. So terribly sorry."

"Does my mom miss me?"

"She misses you every second of every day."

"But she's not sad?"

"She's a little sad. That's why you should go home."

"But where would I wake up?"

The door opened again; Mother came in with a plate of small sandwiches, cut in four pieces.

"But these are tomato sandwiches," I said. "He doesn't like tomato sandwiches."

Simon took the plate.

"I have to go out for a second. Will you stay here?" she said.

"Of course."

She hesitated. "Are you sure?"

"I'm not going anywhere."

"Then I'll be back in a bit. Be good, little Simon."

"Goodbye, Grandma."

"I won't be long."

We heard the front door slam, the sound of a key in the lock.

I said, "Simon, do you think you could go to sleep now?"

"Now?"

"If you go to sleep and I go to sleep, right here, at the same time, maybe we'll wake up together."

"But I'm not sleepy."

"Will you try? I don't have much time."

"Where will we wake up?"

"Maybe the same place. Will you try?"

I took down a blanket and two pillows from the cupboard (it smelt like fresh pine) and spread the blanket under us on the floor. "Now put your head down," I said. "Put your head down and close your eyes." I pulled him tight against me, his little back to my chest, I could feel his small ribs, smell his hair, his creamy skin.

I said, "Tell me something. Just one little thing about your day before I go to sleep."

He said, "I can't think of anything."

"Try."

"I made my own monster today."

"Yeah?"

"Out of Kleenex and cans and some string and a marker for the face."

"What are you going to do with it?"

"I don't know."

"No?"

"Maybe for the puppet show on Friday."

After a moment, I said, "Simon, I'm not in the way here, am I?"

"I like it when you're here."

"You do?"

"I sleep better," he said.

I'm not sure how much later I woke up. The room was dark.

"Simon," I whispered. My arm shot out. He wasn't there but it was warm where he'd lain. I thought, He must have got up to go to the bathroom; I'll just lie here and wait for him to come back. But I don't feel well, I must be getting the flu, *turista* maybe, you get it in the tropics.

When I woke up again, his place was cold, sunlight crept under heavy curtains. The *turista* had clicked in another notch.

"Simon?" I said, but even as I said the words, I knew he was gone, that he hadn't come back with me. For a moment I lay there thinking, I'll go back to sleep, we'll try again. I imagined it was like sinking a bucket into a well, lowering it and bringing it up, lowering it and bringing it up until one time he'd be in it.

Then I remembered. I went into Jessica's bedroom. I said, in the voice of a crippled man, "Can I talk to you for a moment?"

"I'm asleep," she said. Her room smelt like pastel colours, orange and pink and yellow.

I said, "You told me to fix him."

"I did *not* say to fix him, Roman. He's sixty-five years old."

"Can you come down the hall for a minute." I went into the kitchen. A neat, cheerful place. Magnets on the fridge, a photo of Jessica and her mother on a sunny patio somewhere; a succinct little coffee grinder; no crumbs on the counter. I sat down. She came down the hall in a long T-shirt, her hair parted in the middle, paler than I remembered, and sat on the edge of a chair.

I said, "Where was that photo taken?"

"Greece," she said without looking.

"Is that lipstick his idea?"

"Huh?"

"Your mother's lipstick. She'd be very attractive without all that lipstick."

"I have to go back to sleep, Roman," she said.

"Did you hear what that guy said? My *recent sadness*."

"You shouldn't have hit him."

"Guys like that——"

"He's a fuckhead, everybody knows it. That's not the issue."

"What is the issue?"

"This is bullshit, Roman. It didn't used to be bullshit but it is now."

"What is?"

She looked at the ceiling and sighed. "Your situation."

"What do you mean?"

"It's six o'clock in the morning."

I said, "Do you have anything to drink here?"

"I'm going back to bed," she said.

"Jessica."

"I have to get more sleep," she said. "I'm going to feel like shit all day otherwise." You could hear her slippers dragging on the wood floor as she went down the hall. "You should too." Bedroom door eased to without another word.

I went down the hall and stood in front of her door. I said, "I'm feeling pretty terrible about this, Jessica."

"I'm going to sleep now, Roman," she said.

"I don't even know how to get out of here."

"Through the kitchen," she said. "Goodnight."

"Should I lock it behind me?"

No answer. I waited a few minutes longer in the kitchen. I thought she might have second thoughts. And then I left.

The streets seemed particularly ugly that morning; so did the people in them, plastic snouts for faces, barely concealed animalisms. The taxi driver looked at me menacingly when I asked him to turn down his dispatcher's radio. At a red light my eyes rested on a man with an unhealthy tan. He was standing in front of a variety shop, finishing a bag of potato chips. He squeezed the bag into a ball and threw it onto the sidewalk. When he caught me staring at him, he glared back, as if to say, What are you going to do about it, bub? "Save me from all this, Simon," I whispered.

By the time I got back to the hotel I was so anxious I was almost in tears. I hurried through the lobby with my head down. It was one of those mornings you always run into someone you haven't seen for ages, someone who's thrilled to see you, wants to stand very close to you, get a good look at you after all these years. I made it to the elevator, I pushed the button, I was seconds from being home free when I heard my name called merrily across the lobby. It was the night manager, Mr. Hart, an effeminate, balding man with lovely suits. He wouldn't let you go without a clever remark. He hurried over.

"There was a policeman here last night," he said.

"Oh?"

"He was asking about you."

"Really?"

"He asked if you had a girlfriend."

"If I had a *girlfriend?*"

"Of course I wouldn't tell him even if I knew." He looked at me sympathetically. "I said I rather thought not."

"That was considerate of you."

"He also wanted to know if you stayed here every night. If you left on foot or took taxis."

"Plump guy, greasy hair?"

"Very badly dressed," Mr. Hart said.

"I know him."

He lowered his voice with conspiratorial pleasure. "There was a mention of other things."

"There was?"

"Anything that might be perceived as a problem. Erratic behaviour. So on and so forth." This in a whisper.

"That's an easy one," I said.

"I asked him if he wanted to speak to you personally. He said no, not right now."

"Thank you, Mr. Hart."

"I thought you should know."

"Thank you, Mr. Hart."

"Puts a little spice in the evening."

"I'm sure it does."

I got into the elevator; I went up the eighteen floors without interruption, hurried along the hall, afraid to catch even the maid's eye. What was this terror? Why was I so frightened? What could I possibly fear at this stage of the game? But I could feel a cautionary hand on my heart, a touch that said, There are terrible consequences just around the corner.

I took down the bottle of morphine tablets (tucked in behind the mouthwash), shook one into my hand and drank it down with a glass of water. I pulled the curtains and lay down on the couch. A few indecisive minutes later, the pill came on; I could feel the tendons in my back letting go, as if they were coming unstuck. I thought, What is this fuss about? A punch? People were getting punched all over town last night. I sighed. Closed my eyes. Knew what to do. Rest here a bit, then phone Jessica, say some necessary things, this and that. Strange I should feel optimistic about Simon this morning. *My recent sadness.* Who wouldn't have given him a smack? And gradually the horror of it, Jessica's pale face, Morley flying off the chair, the boy in the baseball cap, faded into a kind of reassuring pudding. A face here, a word there, sliding under the surface.

When I woke up, the light was wrong. I lay on the couch, wondering, What is wrong with that light? It seemed hard, rather matter-of-fact light. Impossible, I thought, to explain how a certain kind of sunlight can depress you. Makes you sound like an eccentric. *He claims the sunlight depresses him. No, correct that,* some *sunlight depresses him.* What a solitary business, all this. How much of a relief (let's be candid) to toss it in, to be released from the stress of it. Because solitude *is* a sensation, a kind of hanging dead weight in the middle of the chest. Why would one cling on and on and on by one's fingertips? *Oh, it's you. I'm glad you've come.*

And then I realized what was wrong with the light in my room. It was afternoon light. The interview, the morning interview with the Minneapolis lumber executive. I'd missed it. I was standing over the toilet, trying to pee, trying to remember how to pee, when the phone rang. I snatched it up, mouth dry as flannel.

It was my boss. "Are you feeling any better?" he said.

I couldn't answer. He said, "Jessica told me you're down with the flu."

"It would seem so," I said, turning on the tap and splashing water into my parched mouth.

"My secretary had the same thing last week."

"Really?"

"Just stood up and said, 'I have to go home.'"

"That's it. That's the one."

"The Beijing flu."

"Must be. Hit me like a train."

Pause. "We got Janie to fill in for you."

"How'd she do?"

"Janie's Janie."

"Right."

"She's been groaning for a shot for a year now. So I gave it to her."

"But she was okay?"

"Listen, you and I have to get together," he said.

"Sure. Great."

"You know your contract is up for renewal."

"I'd forgotten."

"How about lunch? My treat. You pick the place."

"Lovely."

You could hear him flapping the page on his day-timer. "How about this Friday?"

"That might be a bit soon. Maybe next week."

"Come and get me in the cafeteria," he said, as if he hadn't heard me. "One-thirty suit you?"

"One-thirty it is."

Rejuvenated by his call, by so close an escape, I called Jessica. I thought, Exploit the momentum. But she didn't take the call. In an editing suite, I supposed, poor Jessica, always in an editing suite. I realized, abruptly, that I wasn't thinking about Simon. I had caught myself, again, on holiday from him, from the sensation of his absence. Like the encounter with the bald man in the theatre, and the dog backing me into a fence, I had sailed, if only for a few moments, out of my condition. Out of my being.

I took the morphine tablets over to the toilet; I was about to pour them out (no more snoozy pills for me), when I stopped. I thought, Let's not be reckless here. You can stop taking them without flushing them down the toilet. You don't have to make a performance out of it. That's addict behaviour. I pulled down the toilet seat and sat, the pills in my hand. My, what a long day it's been and look, only two-thirty in the afternoon. Imagine days of this. Days and days and days and days and days, one after the other, tumbling like circus tumblers, different but irrelevantly so, this one with long arms, that one with a tear in his sleeve, tumbling and tumbling and tumbling. How nauseating.

7

I got into work early that Friday, an attempt, I suppose, at professional engagement. Can't stay away and so on. A job I'd do for free, that kind of thing. There was a new makeup girl, an empty-headed chatterbox who stabbed at my face with her eyebrow pencil as if she were a pointillist. Jessica came in with the script, her tone a tad peremptory, I thought, but maybe I was looking for trouble. The floor director led me through a series of hallways, one after the other, walking just ahead of me, turning his head every so often to ask unfelt questions. On the set, a shaky-handed technician (hungover) pinned my microphone to my shirt and made the same joke he always made, and I caught myself thinking, This is my home.

I got the countdown in my ear, ten, nine, eight, the lights went down, the spotlight came up, I read my introduction from the autocue and brought out the first guest, a window dresser who had once worked for Jacqueline Onassis. The show went without a hitch, moving from item to item; I found myself wishing, cretinously, that my boss was in the control room, that he was witnessing the smoothness with which I went through the gates. Yes, I have had my difficulties, but my technique allows me to perform wind or hail, so to speak.

I remember that show very clearly, a rock star who wouldn't take off his sunglasses, a French anthropologist who claimed cave drawings were a primitive attempt at written language. Which seemed, forgive me for saying it, rather obvious. But apparently I had *mal compris*.

"The drawings," he said, "are not representational. They represent, instead, sounds."

"Sounds?"

On it went.

After the show, I only partially removed my makeup, telling the chatterbox that I was in a dreadful rush; but the truth is, I fancied it made me look rather glamorous, that this might indeed be a good day for it. I surfaced a few feet from the cafeteria and looked in for my boss. He was sitting at a table of admiring producers, sucks, all of them, going on about something, perhaps how television, at its best, was like trying to sell Proust in the chicken market (he was fond of that one).

I opened the door and waited in the entrance to catch his eye.

"We're just finishing up here," he said. I motioned that I'd wait outside, which I did, passing the time with the sports announcer with whom I'd gone house hunting. His manner was breezy, not a splinter in either eye about the missing pills. I realized I hadn't heard from the police, though, no update in more than two weeks. I wondered if they were contacting M., that they'd written me off as a sleaze and a fuck-up and had decided to do business only with an adult.

But they were moving on. You could pretend to yourself they weren't but you could feel it, a somewhat automatic tone in their voices. Checking. Running down a list. There was yet another missing child on the milk cartons. (Who is stealing all these little boys?) I thought, Whoever has him must think they've gotten away with it. They'll get sloppy now, leave him in a backyard, take him to the wrong park. They'll be used to him now, his talkativeness in the morning, his strange staring into the middle distance; they'll know what he likes to eat, what he likes to watch on television. I thought, If he's stopped asking for his parents, it's not because he's stopped missing them, it's because he knows there's no point in asking. I thought, He's a bright boy, he'll know to lie still and wait. If God wants me to believe in him, he will lead me to my son. If he doesn't, fuck him. Fuck him and I will have solved the great mystery of religion. But I don't need to solve the great mystery of religion. Don't be discouraged, I'll find you.

Smelling of tobacco, my boss poked his amiable face out of the cafeteria door. The producers fluttered behind him, saying goodbye, heading back to their offices, visibly uplifted. A man of vision, honey, you should have heard him. Just *incredible*!

He said, "Instead of traipsing all over town, why don't we just fetch a little something here?"

"Where?"

"In the cafeteria." He kept his hand on the door.

I said, "Sounds good."

We went to the same table he'd just left. "Are those new glasses?" he said.

"No. I've had them for, I don't know, a while."

"They look new."

"Nope."

He steepled his hands in front of his face, like a church, collecting his thoughts. Then, a minor distraction, like a housefly. "You're not going to get anything?" he said, jerking his chin toward the sandwich bar.

"No, I'm fine."

"A coffee?"

"I'm good."

Fingers steepled again. "How do you think the show is going?" he asked.

I said, "Fine."

No smile. Brow furrowed. Thoughtful pause. He opened his mouth to speak, but I got it in first. I said, "Why don't we just get right to it."

He nodded solemnly, a quick glance at me, then back to the steeple. "Roman," he said, "you are an acquired taste. And our audience is not acquiring it."

I wish now I hadn't laughed, it was an unbecoming sound, a hyena bark.

He went on. "Here's what I'd like to do. With your permission, that is. I'd like to finish the season, that's what, three, four weeks away?"

"Something like that."

"Then draw up a press release. Say you're moving on to other challenges. Word it any way you want." He paused and looked at me. "I know, under the circumstances, that this isn't what you'd hoped to come from today's meeting."

I said, "What if I quit right now?"

"I don't follow."

"Right now, this minute."

He brushed a speck from the knee of his trousers. "We're all professionals here."

I said, "Where's Jessica?"

"I don't know. Somewhere. Why?"

"Does she know about this?"

"She's sick about it." He bit the inside of his cheek thoughtfully. "Here's what I can do," he said. "We're going to need to audition a whole bunch of people over the summer. You could do the auditions. We could write it into your contract. Full pay. All summer."

I said, "You want me to audition the guy who's going to take my job."

"I'm just trying to keep the wheels on the wagon here, Roman."

A cloud of cigarette smoke slowly revolved at the other end of the cafeteria. I thought, I wonder if it's the sunlight that makes the smoke dance like that. I said, "I'm going to take a walk."

"Does that mean yes?"

I got to my feet. I said, "No. It doesn't."

I went out the fire door. One of the women who worked in the cafeteria smiled at me when I walked by.

She'd lent me five dollars once when I'd forgotten my wallet upstairs.

When I got back to my hotel room, there was a message from Jessica. She asked me to be patient, said that maybe the boss had gone off half cocked, hadn't thought things through. This delivered with a chuckle as if she was on my side. She had a plan, she said. How about if I stayed on till next Christmas? Then we'd have a look at the ratings, sit down like a family, talk about where to go next. *Like a family?* Jessica knew better than that. I wondered if she was in the room with him. Showing off her crisis-solving virtues, the little cunt.

Come back, they were saying, don't fuck us. But there was a sensation in this rupture of having been sent careening down an alley I would go down only at the end of someone's boot. An alley, nevertheless, that I should go down. I lay on my bed watching the clouds pass by the window. I felt it again. I was on the threshold of something. That I should stop resisting and simply abandon myself to it.

So that same night, after midnight, I went over to the studio on foot. I went up the back stairs because I didn't want to run into anybody, didn't want to have to explain. I knew that in spite of myself I'd feel compelled to put on a performance, make a little speech, take the high road, my heart beating like a rabbit's. It gave me a certain pleasure to think of the bunch of them sitting in a hot stew with no host for their show. They could use Janie, naturally, but she was virtually retarded, had complained for years that her good looks prevented her from getting ahead in television; no one took her seriously, she claimed. The fact is, it was only her good looks that got her a job in the first place.

I was dumping the stuff from my desk into a hotel laundry bag when I heard a door open, traces of conversation in the hall. I looked out. It was Jessica, coming out of an editing suite. I opened my mouth to say something but I stopped. She was fiddling with an earring and smiling privately to herself. Then the door opened behind her and someone else came out. It was a cameraman in a beat-up leather jacket.

Jessica looked up, and when she saw me, the expression on her face told me I had, again, misunderstood everything.

8

When I got back to my hotel room later that night, I tossed the laundry bag in the cupboard. I knew I wasn't going to want to see it crumpled on the floor in the morning, that it would have acquired a nasty symbolism by then. I watched television for a few hours, interested, surprisingly, in the news, in a movie I'd previously written off as junk. I felt, I think, clear headed, as if I had wiped down the table, so to speak, that I was now ready, now available. I read the first chapter of a novel I'd loved as a child; a few weeks before I'd seen it in a second-hand bookstore and snatched it up greedily.

Then I turned out the light, my head facing the windows and the world outside, the curtains open. I heard a car honk eighteen floors down, I heard a woman's voice in the hallway, I even thought I smelt perfume, and then blam, I was gone, walking up that cobblestone street. It was a hot night in the tropics; you could hear the fiesta on the other side of town. I noticed a plump man with greasy hair standing in a doorway, smoking a cigar. He was wearing a noisy tourist shirt, a turquoise rag with mariachi singers. He must have bought it at the airport. Without even touching it, you knew it didn't have a shred of real cotton in it.

I said, "What are you doing here?"

"I got some time off," he said. You could tell he'd been drinking.

I said, "Did you follow me down here?"

"What are you talking about?" he said. "I'm on vacation."

I said, "Well I don't have time to talk to you anyway."

He said, "You think I give a shit about a guy stealing a few pills."

That stopped me. "What did you say?"

"Where're you going?" he said, taking a puff on the cigar.

I said, "I'm going to see somebody."

"Mind if I tag along?"

"I do, as a matter of fact. It's personal."

That didn't impress him. In fact, it appeared he'd been waiting for me to say it. "You're out of luck, bub," he said.

I said, "What do you mean, out of luck?"

He said, "You've used up all your visits."

"Says who?"

His moist, thick lips spread with anticipatory pleasure. "You don't think you can just drop in here any time you want, do you?"

"I have to go now, I'm short on time."

As I walked away, he said, "There are rules, you know." I kept walking. "That's the thing with people like you. They don't think the rules apply."

And then I woke up. Another honk from way below my hotel window, exactly the same as the one before. Somebody locking their car, my dream falling between honks. I snuggled down, but I was wide awake. It was as if I'd slept the whole night, as if I had no business being in bed.

Don't force it, I thought. There's no rush. Go back tonight; go back tomorrow night. No difference. I clicked off the reading lamp. By daybreak, that rich light you only see from hotels crept across the city. It spread over the racetrack, the university campus, the parliament buildings; it was moving toward a part of the city I hardly knew, a zone where sometimes you saw blood on the sidewalk. A jogger circled an oval track, around and around and around (how repetitious life is), me standing naked at the window, thinking, There's nothing to get angry about. Sleep will come, sleep will come, sleep will come.

I put a Do Not Disturb sign on the door, I pulled the curtains, I listened to the man next door wake up (clock alarm), take a shower (very faint), then watch a perky morning talk show while he dressed. Then bang, door slammed, keys jingling, he left for the day, and the whole hotel fell silent as a tomb. I didn't go back to the Caribbean, though. I went to Paris. I said to the customs agent, "I think I got on the wrong plane."

"Vous dites quoi?" he said without a trace of a smile.

Nobody called from the show. I've quit jobs before, I know how it goes; still, under the circumstances I was a bit surprised. That same afternoon, I was sitting glassy-eyed in a café in Yorkville when I saw the anchorman for the suppertime news. He was a nice guy, I liked him, even though when he talked to you, even in the elevator, he talked in a big broadcaster's voice. To my irritation I found myself rehearsing a little speech, how everything was okay, how I was glad to be gone, but I didn't need it because when he spotted me he dropped his glance like an anvil and crossed over a half block away. I don't suppose you can blame him. He had his eye on a career move and he didn't want to be spotted with someone from the wrong team.

But the days were long. Stripped of structure they felt endless; I woke up at the same time every morning, just after ten, and made a cheese omelette with three eggs.

"You keep eating all that cheese, you're going to have a heart attack," the woman at the supermarket told me. I thought, Fine.

Then I went for a walk up Yonge Street, but I got only as far as that intersection at Davenport where suddenly, mysteriously, it turns depressing; the street too wide, too much open space perhaps. Then I turned around and came slowly back down to a similar point just below Queen, another corner where inexplicably all possibilities seem to dry up. How do you explain that to somebody?

I came home but it wasn't even lunchtime yet. I watched television. Near noon, I could feel my heart speed up, my hands get sweaty. I couldn't help it. For the first few days, I channel hopped over my show, but then the third morning I thought, Fuck it. You'll never guess what. Janie wasn't sitting in my chair. My boss was. My fucking boss. A few months before he'd disappeared on a holiday, a couple of weeks in St. Lucia. When he came back, he looked younger; sitting there in the morning production meeting, his face pulled on like a tight sock, everyone thinking, My, he looks so refreshed. Jessica said he must have got laid. But that didn't sound right. Then you realized what it was: he'd had a facelift. A little pull-in right there behind the ears. I thought, This is a foul world I wouldn't mind leaving at all.

He wasn't bad on air, to tell you the truth. Watching him do an autocue introduction, interview a guest, I had a feeling that maybe I wasn't as good as I thought I'd been. Or put it this way: that maybe being good on television wasn't as rare a talent as I'd fancied it was. Just because you're an asshole doesn't mean the camera doesn't like your face.

Then I had a tuna sandwich (the pollutants will kill you, dear) and a nap. I didn't go back to the Caribbean then, either. I went to New York with a film crew, I went to Amsterdam with my boss, I went to Holland, those beautiful flowers, with Jessica, I went to my childhood home with M. But never to the Caribbean. I thought, You're being teased. Don't play.

I woke up in the afternoon and stared out the window and had conversations with Simon in my head. Had conversations with M. too. Had conversations with old high-school teachers, old girlfriends. It was extraordinary how vivid my memory was, how I could remember things that were said twenty-five years before. Not important things either, sometimes just phrases. Little apple slices falling into a bucket.

What then? Ah, dinner. I had dinner at that French bistro at the foot of the hill and went to a little jazz joint and drank and then staggered up a street and down a street but I couldn't hear anything. It was as if Simon had pulled the cord out of the wall that connected him to me. Maybe he tripped on it, maybe somebody moved a chair, but I couldn't feel him anymore.

I called M. She'd gone to work for a public relations company right in the centre of the city. I didn't give her a chance to be disappointed. I said, right off the bat, "I don't have news."

There was a silence and then she said, "How are you?"

It wasn't much but it was a shred of warmth, as if she'd let me rest my head on her shoulder for a second, and I started crying.

I said, "I'm so sorry. I'm sorry."

She didn't hang up and even that seemed comforting.

I said, "Have you heard from the police?"

"Nothing," she said.

"But you've heard from them?"

"Yes. Every few days."

I said, "They never call me," and then I was sorry I said it.

"It's not a competition, Roman." Then, realizing I didn't need another boot, she said, "It's a question of manpower, I imagine."

But I was so grateful to talk to her, even for those minutes, that I gulped down her presence like oxygen. And when she said, finally, "I have to go," I said, "Thanks for talking to me."

She said, "I have to go."

I felt like I had some wind in my sails, I felt like I'd touched land, that there was something under my feet, that things were again possible. I didn't even put a name on it. I just felt it. I called the police.

I asked for the greasy-haired cop. He wasn't there, but twenty minutes later he called me back. I said, "I want you to keep me up-to-date about my son."

He said, "I thought we were."

I said, "No, you're keeping my wife up-to-date."

He said, "It's a question of manpower."

Had they worked that out together?

I said, "I want to be included."

There was a long pause. I got ready for things to

escalate. I realized in that half second that I'd been afraid of this guy, that if I was rude to him, maybe he wouldn't look so hard for my son. But then he said, quite calmly, "How you doing?"

It caught me off guard. I said, "Fine. Thanks." It was a morning of surprising warmth.

He said, "I hear you quit your job."

"How'd you hear that?"

"Can't remember," he said. "Must have been on the news."

A joke. He was actually making a joke.

I said, "I don't know your name, officer."

"Raymond," he said.

"Raymond, do you have some kind of a life, other than just following me around?"

He thought that was funny, too. He said, "So what are you going to do, Roman?"

"Don't know."

"Any plans to leave town?"

"Why?"

"Just curious."

"Are you going to come on vacation with me, Raymond?"

"Not the way you guys travel. Couldn't afford it."

I said, "No, no plans to leave town."

9

––––––––––

It was a few weeks now since I'd left the show, early summer but still a chill in the air. People complained about it on the radio. *"What's with this weather!"* I don't know why it happened that particular night, but it did. It was after three in the morning, I lay my head down on the pillow, I slept for a little over fifteen minutes and then my eyes popped open. That was the last time I slept for days. It was just gone, this sense of sleep, of being drawn down into it. It was like a place I had forgotten how to get to.

I turned on the bedside light and returned to the novel from my childhood, the point where the boy steals into the dark castle. My eyes sank; my thoughts unstuck themselves from me and moved off like a herd of small deer. You could watch them from here. A tail flicking; a snort, a start of false alarm; settling back down. I thought, I'm falling asleep.

I closed the book; I said a few comforting words to the darkness. I closed my eyes; I started my descent; the deer moved off again. I was almost home free. Descending and descending. I am falling asleep, I could feel myself almost touching the sandy bottom when the awareness of it, the importance of it, jerked me to the surface. A kind of lightness filled my head as if I'd been plucked from a sunny street. *What am I doing here, in bed?*

I should have got up, they say that; I should have tidied my kitchenette or kept reading or gone downstairs to the lobby. There was nothing to be gained by pulling off band-aids in the dark; nothing to think about, nothing new or productive, just the same exhausted movie of me going down the snowy street, having the beers, smiling at the girls in the band, coming back home, the smell of him in the house, the empty bed. I'd thought about it so many times you could see the sunspots in the film.

I gave up after daybreak, the light coming under the curtains, you couldn't keep it out, no matter what. As if your tent had been packed up and put away for another interminable eighteen hours.

I got up.

For three days this went on. I can't remember what I did, only a series of coloured panels, sitting in a movie theatre, yes, I recall that, although I've forgotten what the film was. Only that I had to change seats several times, once because a woman was eating popcorn so loudly it felt as if she was poking me with a knitting needle. (When the popcorn was gone, she started in on a bag of mints.) I remember sitting in that French bistro. I'd gone there for dinner but just above my head, pointing down at me, was a distractingly bright light, and when I asked the waiter to turn it down, she said no, she couldn't, that the other patrons wanted to see their food, which seemed rather harsh, rather pointed to me, and I left, the menu still on the table. For an hour I fumed about it, about her tone of voice, that slightly irritable dismissiveness. What else did I do? Oh yes. Let me tell you how that came about.

That third morning, bedraggled and red eyed, a foul taste in my mouth as though I were rotting from the inside, I dragged myself down the hall and into the elevator. The sunlight was intolerable. How flat sunlight can be. How disappointing. I wandered here and there like a man trying to get comfortable in bed. A doughnut shop. Too garish, the overheard conversations of incommunicable stupidity.

It was cold too (*What's with this weather!*), the sky blue one minute, the colour of old silverware the next.

So I came back to the hotel and got a scarf, put it around my neck. You could hang yourself with a scarf like that. For a second I lay down on the bed; I almost tricked myself to sleep, drifting along the carpeted hallway of a hotel somewhere, the lights very low, walls royal blue, everything muffled. I thought, It's going to happen, it's going to happen, I'm going to fall asleep. I picked a room. I thought, I'll just sneak in here and lie down. The maids can wake me up; no one'll care. But when I opened the door, the room glowed with electric light, it was like a television studio, people milling about, and I thought, You'll never get to sleep here. Then I was awake again. My brain said, Nice try, pal, but no cigar. Even the voice in my head was starting to sound like a carnival barker.

The cleaning woman knocked on the door and let herself in. "Oh," she said.

I fled back outside. Some kid near the Eaton Centre offered to sell me some pot. "Grow up," I said and kept going. If I go on like this, I thought, I'm going to end up in a fist fight. I went into a greasy spoon and ordered breakfast, eyeballs swimming in a pool of grease. The waitress dropped my toast on the floor. "Do you want jam with that?" she said, putting it back on my plate.

I ate almost nothing, and when I paid at the cashier,

I had to wait while they changed a roll of paper deep in the cash register. The manager came over to supervise, a stubby little Greek with a moustache. Seeing me sigh, he shrugged.

I said, "Maybe you should take care of this stuff on your own time." I left a ten-dollar bill on the counter and stormed out. Then felt queasy about the wasted money, about money in general. It was running out; it was as if I was hemorrhaging money. Soon I'd have nothing to protect me. As I left the restaurant, laughter erupted behind me. Savages. Hardly housebroken and they let them prepare meals for human beings. Sneezing and running their hands through their hair, detritus raining down on meal after meal. Unthinkable bestiality.

I went back into the restaurant. "Don't you care you're killing people with this food!" I said.

More laughter.

I looked up Yonge Street. I could feel myself spilling into panic. What should I do? Where should I go? What should I do? I couldn't go back to bed, couldn't lie there in that daylight, daylight in a minor key, listening to the cleaning women gabbing to each other, the carts rattling by, doors slamming, why do they slam the doors, televisions going on all around me. Why so many needle pricks in a day? I couldn't sit in the lobby, either. I'd done that the day before, Mr. Hart appearing soundlessly at my elbow. Nothing to be alarmed about, he assured me, the network had rung up. Yes? Been something of a change in personnel, apparently. Indeed. No hurry on this, of course, but might be a good time to do a bit of renegotiating. Which meant I had to start paying. Which I couldn't afford to do. *Ten dollars wasted on that appalling breakfast.* Sickening.

I went to a strip joint after that, not because I craved the bodies (although I was surprised how lovely they were, how young and fit) but because of the darkness, the soothing darkness. I had been there only a few minutes when Raymond appeared.

He said, "I thought you guys on TV got a lot of pussy."
I said, "What?"
"I didn't expect to find you in a place like this."
"What can I do for you, Raymond?"
"I was just in the neighbourhood. Saw you duck in here. Thought I'd come by, say hello."
"I didn't duck in here, Raymond."
"Just an expression," he said.
"The maid's cleaning my room," I said. "They don't like it if you stick around."
"I wouldn't know about that," he said. He watched the girl on the stage for a full minute, hands in his pock-

ets, tummy hanging over his belt. "Why don't you just tell me where you put him?" he said. I was so tired, I wasn't sure I heard him correctly.

I said, "What did you say?"

He leaned over and shouted in my ear. "Why do they have to play the fucking music so loud?" Then he pulled back his head and twirled a finger around his ear.

"Right," I said.

He said something else, I couldn't make it out, and then made his slovenly way toward the sunlight outside. A dishevelled bear leaving the cave. I suddenly imagined winter, imagined the dying snow, the hard light, the short days, the bundled faces, the interminable trudging forward.

The waitress came by with a clutch of folded bills between her fingers. I asked for a beer but it was intolerably expensive. What a wastrel I'd become, throwing money here and there, nothing finished, nothing accomplished. Mother, make me lie down; Mother, make me sleep. Say Roman, go to sleep now, and I will. Point me in the right direction, Mother, tell me how to sleep again. Remind me. Just the first few bars.

I was out on the street again, walking north this time, up through a neighbourhood I didn't know. A little enclave somewhere northwest of St. Clair, a few stores, a bank, a grocery store, a little hardware store, very chic. It must have been a neighbourhood for rich people. Those cunts. I stopped in front of a bank. I was looking in the window, I could see the tellers moving around behind the glass, fish in an aquarium. Coarse-eyed fish. A sharp wind slashed through the trees overhead. I thought, I can't stand this, I can't stand another second of this.

I put on a pair of sunglasses; I pulled the scarf up over my mouth (you could hang yourself with a scarf like this); I could feel it easing now, could feel it pulling away from me, like the skin on your back against a car seat; it holds for a second and then lets go; the nausea retreated.

I went into the bank, the room strikingly lit. An arena of lightness. I surveyed the counters; instinct told me to pick the pretty teller. I coughed again into my handkerchief. Kept it over my mouth in anticipation of another cough.

"Good heavens," she said. She stooped like many tall girls, her thick hair pulled behind her ears. I thought, She would be more beautiful with her hair down. I took a withdrawal slip and started to write. The paper slipped. She put down a pair of thumbs; a kindly smile.

I wrote. THIS IS A ROBBERY; GIVE ME ALL YOUR FUCKING MONEY.

Then I drew a line through FUCKING. Too aggressive. When she turned around the note, the smile stopped. She looked at me. I thought, Yes, I can feel this, I can feel this sensation. I saw a woman come in the bank door, I saw a kid looking through his backpack, I saw the manager get to his feet and start down the aisle behind the counter. I thought, There is time for everything. The manager was moving down the aisle, a short man with a face like a baseball mitt. He stopped behind my teller, tilting his head to read something on her desk. It seemed as if he was trying to overhear us. I looked at the teller. Her lips were moving but I couldn't hear what she was saying. I shook my head. Just moving her lips, she said it again, "Just a minute."

I thought, God has sent me my lady of the flowers. God has sent me my salvation.

The manager turned around and headed down the aisle. The teller, still stooped, opened the cash register and scooped out three packs of bills. She left the bottom one where it was. She said, very softly, "Dye pack."

She put the money on the counter. I put the bills in my inside breast pocket, one pack, two packs, three packs, and then I walked very slowly out of the bank.

I didn't look back. I knew she was there, that she was watching over me, that the manager was at his desk, that the kid was still fiddling with his backpack. I knew all this without turning around. I thought, as the sunlight hit me out on the street, I love it here. I must stay here.

I was just about to slide down into the subway when a police car pulled over abruptly. Down went the window. I thought, Oh, this is how the end feels.

But the cop said, "When are you going to have some real cops on your show?"

I said, "I beg your pardon." I looked up the street. I was only three blocks from the bank.

He said, "You get all those guys who *play* cops, why don't you get the real thing?"

I said, "We should, yes."

His partner, who was a bit older and driving, looked over. He said, "What's Richard Gere like?"

I said, "A bit of an asshole."

The younger cop said, "He's the Buddhist, right?"

"Whatever," his partner said, lifting up his arm and putting it on the seat rest. "He was pretty good in that film."

"The one where he played a cop?"

"Yeah, that one. I hear he wanted the part in *Misery* but they didn't even consider him."

"Huh?"

The younger cop said, "Was that the movie where they chop the guy's feet off?"

"No," I said, "that's the book. In the movie, they just hobble him."

A taxi pulled up behind the squad car. I signalled him.

"No," the older cop said, "they were better with that other guy. The guy from *The Godfather*."

"Jimmy Caan," I said.

"Jimmy Caan. Now there's a guy with a pair."

The cab driver flashed his parking lights. "I have to go, guys."

The older one said, "You ever interview Dean Martin?"

I looked down the street; still nothing in front of the bank. I said, "No." I took off my jacket and folded it on the sidewalk in front of where I was crouching.

"You know the story about Dean Martin?" he asked his partner.

"No, I don't know that one."

The cop said, "This guy wants to interview Dean, right? And Dean says, I'll tell you what, I won't interview *you* if you don't interview *me*."

"Fuckin' Dino," his partner said. In the corner of my eye, down in the direction of the bank, I saw a flourish, some motion, but I didn't look. Suddenly the young cop sat forward and punched a button on his computer. "We got to go," he said.

I tucked my jacket under my arm and went to the taxi and got in. I said, "Follow that police car, will you? I'm with them."

"I'll need an address," the driver said.

"Just do it, please."

When I got back to the hotel, I fell asleep with my shoes still on, the money still in the inside pocket of my jacket thrown over a chair. I found Simon sitting by a pond near the centre of town, his hands under his legs. His legs swinging. He was wearing khaki shorts and the red sandals. I sat down beside him. In the middle of the pond, a man younger than me, I thought I recognized him, was leaning over a very small child, releasing a sailboat.

I said, "Simon, do you ever dream?"

He thought about that for a second, swinging his legs. "No," he said. "Do you?"

"All the time."

"What do you dream about?"

"You. I dream about you," I said.

"Are they nice dreams?"

"They're wonderful dreams. They're better than anything."

We watched the man with the boat; he and his son were wading through the shallow water, the little boy batting the boat, his dad smiling and gently restraining his small hand.

"I hate it there, Simon," I said. He turned a small, worried face toward me. I said, "Don't worry. I'm going back."

"Is my mother all right?"

"She is."

"Does she ever go into my room?"

"Yes, she does."

"Why doesn't she ever come?" he said.

"I don't know. But she wants to."

"Then why doesn't she?" he said. I remembered suddenly how little he was.

"Because she doesn't know how," I said.

"You know how."

"Yes," I said, "but I don't know how I know."

After a moment he said, "You can come here now, Daddy."

It took me a few seconds to understand. I said, "You mean to live?"

He nodded. There was a hint of mischief in his face.

"I don't have to go back?"

He shook his head.

I said, "Are you sure? I wouldn't get in the way or anything?" I put my hand on his small cheek. "This is the best news I've ever had, Simon."

"It is?"

"In my whole life."

We watched the father and son for a moment. Then a cloud passed over the pond; the water grew dark; a sudden gust of wind ruffled the surface.

"Simon, tell me you won't change your mind, will you?"

"Uh-uh," he said.

"Promise?"

"Promise." He touched my chest with a small finger and then put his hands under his legs again.

"Then we have all afternoon," I said. And indeed we did.

10

It was after four in the morning when I woke up. I was wide awake, completely refreshed. I ate a piece of banana cake right out of the fridge, then another and a big glass of milk. I looked out the window. How beautiful the city looked at night. I realized it had always been beautiful. I was lucky to live here, I thought. So lucky. I turned on the television. How bright the images were, how compelling. It felt as if I'd been away from civilization for months. I wanted to read magazines, watch the news, listen to music. I thought, I'm back in the world.

At five-thirty I called the limousine company. Got the gruff-voiced owner. "Same address?" he said.

"No, it's the Chelsea Hotel."

"The Chelsea Hotel," he repeated writing it down, not asking why after all this time I was at a hotel. Maybe he knew. He said, "Where are you going today, sir?"

I said, "Grenadier."

"What time's your flight?"

"Not sure. I'm trying pot luck."

He said, "Caribbean flights tend to leave early in the morning."

"Right."

"Maybe we should get you right now."

"Sounds good," I said.

"Have a good day, Mr. Roman," he said.

Then I called M. It rang a few times; she must have turned off her answering service in case the police called during the night. I said it quickly so she wouldn't wait for it. I said, "I don't have any news."

I could hear her exhale and lie back down again. I said, "I just wanted to say something to you."

Pause. I said, "I always thought that the great love of my life would be a woman. But I was wrong. It was him. He was the great love of my life."

She didn't say anything for a while. Then she said softly, "I know that, Roman. I've always known that."

"You have?"

"Right from the start."

"Okay then," I said.

"Okay," she said.

"Bye-bye, M."

She waited a few seconds. She was wondering, I think, if there was something she wanted to add, to ask. Then: "Bye bye, Roman."

I took down that blue overnight bag she'd given me for my birthday a thousand years ago. I thought about packing my pillow, they never had feather pillows in the Caribbean, but then decided against it. I went into the bathroom, fished around in the medicine cabinet until I found the morphine pills. I dropped them into the bag, then stood there looking at them. What if they made me check the bag and then lost it en route? I took the pills out and put them in my jacket pocket. A linen jacket, a lovely jacket. They gave it to me on a show a few years back. Instead of a raise. You can have some new clothes, they said, but you'll have to give them back when you leave the show. No one ever gave their clothes back, but they said it anyway.

I put the bag back in the cupboard. I went into the bathroom and brushed my teeth and washed my face. The cold water felt delicious. I looked at myself in the mirror. Not bad. Not bad for a man who never slept. Lost a bit of weight. It suited me. Hard way to lose a few pounds, though.

I was watching the morning news when my phone rang. It was just getting light, a clear blue sky, the sun warming up the trees and the gardens and the playing fields. You fly over this city, you'd swear you were looking down at a forest. A city in a forest. How heartbreakingly beautiful it all was.

I went downstairs. The air conditioner was on in the lobby; the floors had been polished to a high gleam. Mr. Hart stood at the reception desk, a solitary black figure, like a crow on a post a mile away. When I got abreast he looked up.

"Leaving us today, Mr. Roman?" You could see the limo outside, driver smoking a cigarette, the trunk up.

"I'm just going away for a few days."

"Sounds perfect," he said. "A good weekend to get away."

"Indeed."

"You know what they say," he said with a raised eyebrow.

"What is that, Mr. Hart?"

"A change is as good as a rest."

"Indeed it is." I turned to leave.

"What shall I say if anyone inquires after you?"

"No one will," I said with a laugh.

"But should they?"

"Tell them I'm not here."

"Excellent response," he said.

"Goodbye, Mr. Hart."

"The same to you, sir."

It didn't take us long to get to the airport; it was as if we caught every light, made every turn, got every lane change. I said to the chauffeur, "You're a good driver."

Looking at me in the mirror; he was dark skinned, handsome, Sri Lankan maybe. He said, "Thank you, sir."

I said, "Do you like your job?"

"Oh yes," he said.

"Are the people nice?"

"Mostly," he said.

I said, "It's true, isn't it?"

"I beg your pardon, sir?"

"Just that. That most people are nice."

"Oh yes, sir. They are."

He checked in the mirror to see if I wanted to say more but I didn't and we drove through the dazzling sunlight in silence.

Finally I said, "God, it's a beautiful day."

He looked at me with mild surprise as if I had just plucked that very thought from his head. "A perfect day to go to China."

I leaned forward in my seat. "I'm sorry?"

"My mother used to say that. Whenever it was a perfect day, she would open the window and say, 'Why look at that! It's a perfect day to go to China.'" He checked the lane over his shoulder. "I don't know why she said it. We never went to China. Not once, not ever. It was just one of those peculiar things that your parents say."

"That you never forget," I said.

"Exactly, sir." He laughed suddenly. "It makes no sense but still you remember it for the rest of your life."

It is a warm world, I thought. It is a warm world and I have been lucky to live in it.

I went to the Air Grenadier desk. "For when?" the clerk asked. Blue, crisp uniform; delicate features. Only a trace of the early hour on her face. The makeup perhaps a bit resolute.

"This morning," I said.

"Do you have a ticket?"

"I'm afraid not."

"A reservation?" She was looking at the computer screen.

"Plenty of those. But not for this flight."

"It's going to be expensive," she said.

"That's okay."

Quietly smiling. She said, "Spur of the moment?"

"Spur of the moment, indeed." I watched her eyes moving over the screen. "Is there anything?" I said. She could hear the concern in my voice.

"I imagine," she said. "Just give me a moment here." She looked over her shoulder at the clock. "We have one flying into Albertville at nine-twenty."

"Sounds good."

She clicked the keys. "When do you want to come back?"

"Doesn't matter," I said.

Still smiling. "You really *are* getting away."

"You bet."

"But I'm still going to need a date."

"How about next week?"

More clicking. "Saturday good?"

"Perfect. I love coming home on a Saturday."

I paid her in cash.

"Wow," she said. "I haven't seen anyone pay cash for a long time." She had to go to another wicket to get the change. When she came back, she said, "Do you have any luggage today?"

"None."

"Passport?"

"Right here."

She looked at it. "I know you."

A small buzzing sound. She handed me my boarding pass. "Have a good trip," she said.

I bought a bottle of Russian vodka in the duty free and then an Elmore Leonard novel next door. For a second I hesitated. I thought maybe I should get something good for me, but then I thought no, you don't have to think like that anymore.

It was the same thing at the sandwich counter. The girl in the green smock asked me if I wanted butter on my tuna sandwich. I opened my mouth to say no but then I said, "Sure."

"Salt?"

"Plenty," I said.

When she saw me smiling, she said, "You been on a diet?"

"Sort of."

"You look good to me," she said. "Man like you doesn't need a diet."

I thought, The limo driver was right.

I got a seat by the window; normally I sit in the aisle in case I have to get up to take a pee, but this time I wanted to see everything, I wanted to see the city fall away below us. My city, my home, there, up near that clutch of houses near the park, that's my old neighbourhood, that's where I trick-or-treated on foggy nights and went tobogganing and committed minor crimes. I rode my bicycle along those streets. The plane arced over the city, how huge it's grown, the morning sunlight glinting off windshields, miles and miles and miles of cars lined up all the way to the horizon. Over the lake, a sailboat down there, a coal freighter, like a Tony Bennett painting. Who would ever have believed that Tony Bennett was such a good painter?

And then upward, upward and upward. Heading home. Heading home at last. One final backward look at the city, one last scan over the houses and the trees and churches. Those warm stone graveyards. He's not down there anymore. I don't feel him anymore. He's gone.

The stewardess said, "Can I get you some breakfast, sir?"

I thought about it for a second. "No, but you can get me a drink."

"It's too early for bar service."

"Well, if you can get me a drink, great. If you can't, that's great, too."

She came back with a glass of tomato juice and slipped me a tiny vodka bottle. "Don't tell anyone," she whispered.

I dumped the vodka into the glass. I stared out the window, thirty thousand feet now. A fledgling cloud whipped by below, then another, looking for the rest of the herd, I suppose. A lost cloud. I felt the vodka come on; it loosened my neck. I sat back. I closed my eyes.

Someone close to me said, "Is this yours?" A woman sitting on the aisle held up a magazine. Skinny, sharp chin, with the haircut of a well-groomed crow.

"No," I said.

"You never get anything good to read on these planes."

I didn't answer.

"All the good stuff gets taken. People get on the plane, they take the magazines with them when they go."

I took a sip of my drink. "That's right."

"Can you believe it? People taking the magazines with them when they go. Unbelievable."

I could feel a whole set of muscles tightening up. I thought, Don't bother.

"You don't want to talk, do you?" she said.

"No, I don't mind."

"It's just unusual to meet a guy on a plane who doesn't want to talk."

We sat there in silence; how lovely not to have to supply the next sentence. After a while she opened the magazine and started to read. Very ostentatiously. I'm free of all that now, I thought. You can take that chimney stone and lay it on someone else's chest.

She said, "I'm going down to meet my boyfriend. Just in case you have any doubts."

I couldn't help myself. There was something about the insistent nakedness of her feelings that made you want to laugh out loud. "What?"

She said, "I don't want you to think I'm just cruising up and down the plane looking for guys."

"I really didn't think that," I said.

"People get some pretty strange ideas."

When I glanced over again, she was staring straight ahead, as if she were watching a vivid movie in her head, her dry lips slightly parted. She sat back into her seat. I thought, She's getting ready to tell me something. Then she said, "My husband's unfaithful to me. I took his charge card. I'm going to spend all his money."

I said, "I'm sorry to hear that."

She said, "You know what he did?"

I put my hand gently on her arm. I said, "I'm very sorry but I can't talk to you anymore. I hope you're not offended."

When I turned around again, she was sitting in an empty seat a dozen rows down.

11

I've always loved the Albertville airport, this collection
of cement blocks, two storeys high, the floors made of
green putty. Hot as a sauna. Alarmingly hot. People
going "Oh my goodness" when they roll open the plane
door and the *chaleur* comes windmilling up the ramp
to greet them. But it's made me happy to get there so
many times, particularly in my twenties, that my body
can't help but rise to the occasion, to have its own sense
of event. I waited for the woman with the unfaithful
husband to leave first. I waited till everyone left, looking out at the tarmac, the green fields shimmering in
the heat; behind them the ocean, a little green shack
perched at the very edge with a single small window.
I always saw it when I arrived and I always wondered
about it. I thought, I must find out who lives there. But
I never did. I was too impatient to get to the hotel, to

get things started. So this time, I broke away from the file of passengers and started across the tarmac toward it. A black policeman caught me by the elbow. He said, in island French, You go this way. I asked him, in high-school French, who lived in the green shed. He shielded his eyes from the glare.

"That's a tool shed," he said.

"It looks like a little house."

"It's a tool shed for the vehicles that service the planes."

"No one lives there?"

"Not that I know."

"No one even sleeps there?"

"Non."

"Pas de mystère," I said.

"Pas de mystère," he agreed and then nodded toward the cement building. "Vous allez par là."

A little gypsy trio entertained us while we waited for customs, the lead guitarist missing two fingers. You could smell the cigarette smoke drifting through the thick air. People lighting up. Black tobacco. The smell of France. A woman behind me told me how much she'd enjoyed my interview with Frank Sinatra, just before his death. I said, That wasn't me, that was some-one else. But she kept looking at me, this handsome woman in her sixties, red lipstick that reminded me of Jessica's mother, and I realized that the Sinatra interview was a pretext, a slippered foot to stop the door from closing. She said, "I'm terribly sorry about your misfortune."

I said, "Thank you."

She said, "My husband died of leukemia."

I said, "I'm sorry."

She said, not taking her eyes away from me as if I might disappear if she broke contact for even a second, "That's not what I mean."

I didn't say anything. The gypsy band broke into "J'attendrai." The line moved forward.

She said, "When I read about you in the paper, I wanted to write you a letter."

A young black woman in her early twenties, vibrantly dressed, came by with a tray of red drinks with little umbrellas in them. I took one. I said, "Can I get you a drink?"

She didn't take her eyes away. She said, "You know what I learned?"

I said, "Ma'am, I don't mean any offence here—"

"Let me finish," she said with surprising assurance. "I learned that you cannot *imagine* your life in five years."

"I'm sure that's true."

"Please don't brush me away. Listen to me. That's what makes it intolerable, the notion that it's going to stay the same. But I'm here to tell you it doesn't."

"But it could be *worse*," I said after a moment.

"It could. But it won't be the way you imagine it."

The line opened ahead of us. I said, "I'm sorry about your husband."

As if she hadn't heard me. "It's the best argument. It's the *only* argument."

"Against what?"

"You think no one else knows, but I do. I can tell."

We went to different customs booths. I recognized the agent. He was grey haired now, heavier. We always greeted each other. Once, twenty years earlier, I'd made a joke about having a machine gun in my bag and he'd made me wait in the holding area for three hours while all my friends went on.

We shook hands, him very formal, he stamped my passport, asked me if I was going to the same town. I said yes. He asked, A holiday? I said yes. And marriage, he said, how was that? I said, Difficult. It was the right answer for a man with nine children. He said, "You know why I have nine children?"

"Why?"

"Because when I am old and shitting in my pants,

there will be someone to look after me." This delivered deadpan.

The woman with lipstick was still watching me when I stepped out of the airport into the dazzling sunlight; she was frowning, as if she was running the conversation over in her head, wondering if she'd got it, said it right, been clear enough.

I was going to take a taxi but I thought no, I was hungry for bodies squeezed against mine, bodies I could smell, impersonal chatter, the stops to get beer, the driver picking up his girlfriend a few miles outside town. It was only two o'clock; there were hours and hours and hours and hours before nightfall, a whole afternoon, a whole evening. No rush to arrive. I'd made it over the water; now it was like being wound in on a fishing line.

I climbed onto a red van and sat by the window near the back; we stalled for quarter of an hour, smouldering in the full-on sunshine, the driver delaying for a full load, the passengers getting fidgety. (Are we leaving soon? You said five minutes.) I looked out the window at the blazing green, the hills rising over the airport, those tall trees rising above the others. Rising up and bending over toward me. *Come into me.*

And then the door slammed and we took off, a German girl squeezed against me as we turned our way up through the circular streets to the top of the hill and then headed along the coast, the sea below, the white-capped reef, the waves breaking, the German girl perspiring, fanning herself with her visa. How long has it been, I thought, since I've been touched by a body, smelt a woman's sweat? So *this* is life.

"Packed in like fish," she said in breezy English. She had blotches of red in her cheeks like the girl at the funeral. Claire English's daughter. *I'll remember the way you looked, my mommy, not the way you were at the end.* Was that what she said? Something like that. Still, rather harsh. But maybe that was the way they spoke to each other, naked like that, like the woman on the plane.

There were all the stops I imagined: a tall boy, early twenties, disappearing behind a palm tree (he'd drunk too much on the plane); a bearded professor who bought a case of local beer and passed them around; another stop while the driver hunted for a CD of Senegalese rock, the volume from which vibrated the van's skeleton, the passengers nodding their heads. We whizzed down into a gorge, the mountain cupping its hands on each side, the ocean out of sight, a river winding down through the jungle, and beyond it, a red-roofed town.

"It is heaven, yes," said the German girl.

"Let's hope so," I said.

There's such beauty in the world, I thought, such beauty.

It always rained on the way to the hotel and it did this time too. A momentary, subduing note, like students settling down before class. The sky darkened, a shadow hurtled across the cane fields, the rain pelted down, the windshield wipers wiped like a metronome. On the other side of the island, above the ocean, now an inexpressible grey, the grey of drowned sailors, lightning flashed, the sky lit up. The music stopped; a gloomy silence fell inside the van. The passengers solemn, matching the weather, white faces turned to the windows, the water slick under the wheels, the sadness of the tropics; disconsolate children by the side of the road; a half-dressed man walking in circles in a muddy town centre. The driver rounded the corners with a double honk.

Then, reaching the bottom of a glade, we started a slow climb, the driver gearing down, then gearing down again, and when we neared the top, just at the crest, the clouds blew apart, the sun blasted forth, the music came back on, and the passengers, as if they had been frozen, reanimated themselves. I used to think, when we arrived at this point in the trip, Let me live here. When my knees are old, let me come here to die. Let me vanish one warm night into the sea. Vanish without a trace. The rain steamed in puddles, the van roared alongside a beach now, a solitary bather drifting along the lip of the sand. It occurred to me in those few seconds that I'd been working up to this for a whole lifetime.

I tapped the bearded man on the shoulder. "I'll have one of those beers now, if you don't mind."

I checked into the hotel in the late afternoon, that hour when the whole island drips with a kind of golden paint. I had been in my room only a few minutes when the owner, Potz, a small Algerian with a goatee and pale blue eyes, knocked on my door and came in. I hadn't seen him since Simon was a baby, a plump-limbed butterball. At the thought of it, I looked at my watch.

He asked about my family. I said, All good. I asked about business. He said they'd had a bad year. Tumbling into French, he rhymed off the hurricane, a pair of unsolved murders (Australians), a sudden rash of all-inclusive hotels down on the beach. From my window, like a painting, you could see the beach on the other side of the town; behind it, the blue mountains. I used to promise myself, every time the taxi took me back to the airport, that I'd wander around those mountains sometime. Towns where the earth was red and everybody wore sunglasses. From the top of those mountains, I heard, you could see all the way to Cuba.

A lazy man's life.

I said, "Potz, tu fais toujours le péché?" I meant to say do you still fish, but I said instead are you still sinning?

"Comment?" he said. You could see he still had his mistress in town.

I repeated it in English and we both had a laugh about it.

"Yes," he said. "I still fish."

"Toujours le même bateau?"

Yes, he still had his boat.

I asked him if he'd lend me a hundred Grenadarien dollars, which was a joke about me always turning up at the hotel a bit drunk and without the right currency. I'd say, "I missed the bank," and for some reason, good manners perhaps, he found that amusing, year in and year out. He peeled off a string of blue bills from a thick wad. There'd always been rumours about Potz, that he stashed money for drug dealers, that he kept it in a safe in the bar, stacks of American hundreds. Oh, and a gun, too. It gave him an aura that he quietly enjoyed, and American girls, particularly middle-class college students, sometimes went to bed with him.

I said, "How's your son?"

"Good."

"Still in Paris?"

"Bordeaux. Medicine." He pronounced it the French way.

I said, "He's in medical school now?"

"But he's lonely in France. He wants to transfer here. We quarrelled at Christmastime. Medical school not so good here."

I said, "I bet you miss him."

He said, "I told him not to transfer. But he's a very disobedient boy."

I must have had more to drink in the van than I realized because I was suddenly exhausted. When Potz left, I lay down on my bed, the bedspread still on, the curtains lank and motionless in the heat. From there I could see a tree shooting straight up from the jungle. It was the same tree I always looked at when I arrived. There was a bird, a crow, I think, perched right at the very top. I'd never seen a bird in it before. I thought, That must be some view. I heard voices in the room below me, a couple had just come in from a day at the beach. They must have been from the south, maybe Marseille, because they talked very quickly. A lot of slang. I could hardly make it out. I thought, I'll just lie here for a bit; maybe I'll take a walk to the beach later, or maybe go up the road, that bar where people go to watch the sunset, the hornets buzzing around the sugary drinks and making the French girls scream. Maybe not, though. Maybe I'll just lie here until dark.

When I woke up, I could hear the bullfrogs in the moist jungle and a huge moon shone through my window. I looked at my watch; it was nearly eight o'clock. I'd been gone for hours. Sweat dripped down my chest, the mattress wet under me. The curtain still motionless. From the patio at the front of the hotel I heard faint music, the sound of evening voices, the sound of tourists showered and tanned, the first delightful upswing of alcohol.

You couldn't see the tree anymore; it had vanished against the night sky. But I found myself thinking about that crow. I wondered if he was still there, if he knew what a gorgeous rag of an island it was. Or was it just a good place to sit? Then I thought about the woman on the plane. She'd be a pretty woman if it weren't for that hair. I imagined her by now at a table, probably with a man, probably telling him her story, what her husband did, what she caught him doing, how long it had been going on. How she'd taken his credit card and was going to spend all his money. What a good time she was going to have doing it. And yet, there was something appealing about her, her fresh, undisguised pain.

I was hungry, very hungry. And taking my jacket with me, I went down to the patio bar. I thought, I'll come back up later for the Russian vodka. I got a table near the front where I could watch the people passing by on the road just a few yards away, some heading down to the beach, others heading up to the bars. It was Saturday night. A Saturday night in the Caribbean.

The waiter came over, a lanky black man in bistro dress: black pants, white shirt. He brought me a glass of dark rum. It's a present from Potz, he said. He had to go up the road. Which was where his mistress lived. "Vous voulez manger, monsieur?"

I said, "I want to have something I've never had here before."

That puzzled him. He looked at the menu, then at me. He said, "You like lobster?"

I said, "I like the *idea* of lobster. But lobster itself is always something of a disappointment. Do you know what I mean?"

"Comme les pommes," he said. Like apples.

I could feel the first reassuring wash of the rum. I said, "It's true. Apples are rather a disappointment, too." I looked again at the menu. "I'd like an omelette, I think. I'd like it with those big mushrooms."

He wrote it down carefully in French. I said, "It's an unusual thing to have for supper, isn't it?"

He pursed his lips. "Pas tellement."

I said, "I hear they grow in cow patties."

"Monsieur?"

"Those mushrooms, they grow in cow patties."

He understood the cow part. "C'est ce qu'on dit." That accent, so thrown together, so offhand.

"It's not a problem, I'm just curious," I said.

"Et voilà."

"I'll have another drink, too."

I settled back in my wicker chair. There was a table of young Americans near me, one of them red faced from the sun. A French couple, very thin, drinking a bottle of wine and talking quietly. People drifting by on the street, a car, a pair of bicycles, a wobbly man with long hair looking at his feet with great determination. Music suddenly rose up from inside the bar. A Portuguese folk song, a woman's clear lament; and with it I experienced a surprisingly persuasive second gust, an updraft from the rum, and I thought, I'm happy. I always thought it would be worse, more operatic. But it isn't. It is, under this round moon, rather sweet in the end. The woman in the airport was right, the one with the lipstick, you really *can't* imagine anything. I remembered M. sitting on the porch of the lamp store, her saying—

But no, not that, not now. I turned my attention to the street, to the people in summer whites passing up and down. Clothes for a summer's night. Lovely expression, that. I'd heard it somewhere. Where? Doesn't matter.

The waiter came over with the omelette. I said, "I'd like some hot mustard with it."

"Hot mustard for an omelette, monsieur?"

"I used to eat a lot of omelettes when I was a student."

He listened politely.

"And after a while I started putting mustard on them. It got to be a habit and now I can't break it."

He waited to see if there was anything I wished to add, any further non sequiturs. There weren't. Unfolding my napkin and handing it to me, he said, "Et bien, je vous laisse."

"I'll have a coffee and a cognac, please."

I thought, Well, we're almost there. The sky was still clear, the stars bright; a slight wind came up from the ocean across the road. It said, Take your time, but don't tarry.

12

The cognac came. I dumped it into my coffee. I borrowed a cigarette from the Americans and I lit up. I sucked it all the way in and then, exhaling it into the moist air, I saw, on the road just in front of me, a sleek-headed woman. Black linen slacks, sleeveless black top, dangling silver earrings that suited her long face. It was the woman with the unfaithful husband.

"Hello," I said (too loud, heads turned), but she saved me by coming boldly up the stairs and onto the patio. Strange, I thought, vanity, the last thing to go. Like a rattlesnake's tail.

I said, "Can I buy you a drink?"

"I'm on my way to meet some friends," she said.

"Ah, then have a pleasant evening."

"But I could sit down for a moment."

"That would be sensational."

Sensational?

She'd washed her hair; it was fluffier now, less disastrous. The water was soft on the island. It made everybody's hair look good.

"So you're not lonely sitting out here, having dinner by yourself?" she said.

"Not so far."

"Not worried about missing a thing, are you?"

"Nope, definitely not."

The waiter came over. She ordered a beer in very good French. Somehow that hair didn't go with good French. I was going to ask her where she'd learned it but I didn't. I didn't want to waste time. It was better as a mystery. Out of the corner of my eye I saw a noisy shirt go by on the road. Turquoise with red splashes. I thought, Who's that?

"I like your hotel better than mine. I'm on a package deal," she said, looking up at the white facade, the balconies over the bar, one of which nurtured a speechless couple. Hashish, I assumed.

"Ah."

"Sort of a last-minute thing." She was like a patient with a toothache, there was nothing else she could think about.

"So you mentioned."

"Of course, now that I'm here, I'm thinking, now what?" she said.

"Right."

She said, "It kind of gets off the plane with you, doesn't it?"

"Yes, it does."

"Matter of fact, correct me if I'm wrong, it seems to get almost worse." She gave an attractive, rueful laugh.

We stared at the people drifting by on the road.

"You know what I've noticed?" she said.

"What?"

"I've noticed that people who travel a lot——?"

"Yes."

"Never ask any questions. They have no curiosity about anybody. Have you ever noticed that?"

"I have, actually."

"You'd think of all people they'd be curious."

"You would, wouldn't you."

She stared at me for a moment. "So ask me a question."

I said, "Let me buy you a drink. A proper one."

"A proper one, eh?"

"Yeah. And then let's just sit here and stare into space."

She jangled a bracelet on her wrist and then lost interest in it. "Do you mind if I smoke?"

"No, help yourself."

A dog barked up the road; something moved in the vegetation; a car passed.

"This is kind of peculiar," she said. "Someone asks you for a drink and then they ask you not to talk."

"You can talk if you want."

She took another sip of her beer. "You're just not going to pay any attention."

"Mild attention."

I waved the waiter over. "Two cognacs, please."

"Do you mind if I ask you something?" she said.

"Depends."

But she didn't get it out because at that moment an elderly couple stepped off the road and came up the stairs. They were dressed expensively and having a lovely time. An anniversary, maybe. They greeted us in English accents and went into the bar, the man, white haired, putting his hand very gently on the small of his wife's back. They sat in a booth.

The cognac arrived and we sipped it in silence, both of us staring out at the road, and beyond it the ocean.

"This is nice," she said.

"Yes."

"It's nice to have a drink with somebody in a foreign country."

"It is."

"Now I can go back to my hotel and feel like I did something my first night in town." She took a puff of her cigarette, then blew it out thoughtfully. "What's your name?"

I hesitated for a second but it didn't seem worth it. I said, "Roman."

She said, "You're a nice man, Roman. God must have sent you to me."

"Thank you."

"You're my lady of the flowers," she said.

"What?"

The white-haired Englishman rose from his booth, his wife beaming, and went over to the bar. There was something about his movements, the jauntiness of a thoroughly engaged older man, that made me watch him. American dollars were exchanged with the lanky waiter, the music stopped, the man returned to his booth, his wife looking up expectantly; then, with the crackle of an old vinyl record, Edith Piaf began to sing "La Vie en Rose"; the white-haired man raised his wife to her feet, she rested her hand on his shoulder, she looked at him with amusement and tenderness and affection, you have to love someone for many years to look at them like that, and then they had a little sway, not far from their booth, not ostentatious, although everyone in the room now looked at them. The two of them, slightly bent with age, wrinkled hands. I tried to imagine M. and me, thirty, forty years down the road, but what I saw, inexplicably, was a stretch of highway in the country somewhere, just before a bridge, snow skittering along the pavement in the wind.

"Do *you* want to dance?" she said.

I said, "No, not just now, thanks."

"Come on," she said, "for old times sake."

I leaned over and kissed her on the cheek. "I like you," I said, "but I have to go now."

I stepped off the patio onto the road, crossed over without looking back, descending a white sandy path until it disappeared in the forest. Down through the trees, the damp vegetation, zigzagging this way and that way, the smell of the ocean getting stronger, the moon hanging utterly round, utterly neutral overhead. I came out in a clearing, a dark-sanded beach. The tourists never came here; the seashells cut their feet. Near an old log, underneath a pile of dead branches, I found

Potz's canoe. Sometimes, late at night, armed with only a hand line and a giant silver lure hook, he went fishing for barracuda.

I dragged the canoe over the sand into the water, kicked off my shoes and got aboard. I was reaching down for the paddle when I heard something behind me. I thought the woman from the bar had followed me. I thought, Don't be harsh. But it was Raymond. A cop in paradise. In the bright moonlight, I could see his ghastly shirt, the slight gleam to his hair.

I said, "Jesus, what are you doing here?"

He waded out till he was waist high in the warm water and put both hands on the gunnel. I thought he was going to pull me in to shore.

"I'm taking a holiday," he said. "Everybody gets a holiday, why not me?" He kept his hands on the gunnel.

I said, "I saw you earlier."

He looked out at the water, the moonlight rippling all the way to the horizon. "What's on the other side of that?"

"What do you mean?" I said.

"Say you got in a boat and just headed straight out. Where would you end up?"

"China," I said.

"*China?* Are you bullshitting me?"

I said, "Raymond, don't you have a wife or something?"

"Not when I'm on holiday," he said. "You going fishing?"

"No, I'm just going for a little paddle."

"A peaceful little paddle," he said. "Sounds good. Fancy some company?"

I said, "No, not tonight, Raymond. Maybe we could have a drink together tomorrow night. You'll still be here?"

"Rain or shine. Couldn't leave if I wanted to."

"Then I'll see you tomorrow night."

He let go of the boat. "Don't go get yourself eaten by something."

I paddled out for fifty, a hundred yards, the moon dancing on the water, and looked back. Raymond was standing on the shore now, his arms crossed, watching me. I saw the red glow of a cigarette; it may even have been a cigar.

I paddled for twenty minutes and then when I was way out, when I could no longer make out Raymond, when the shoreline was little pricks of glowing light, I pulled the pill bottle from my pocket. I thought, The current will carry me out from here. Then I remembered the vodka. I'd left it in my room. I sat numb for a moment. Not even this, not even this. I poured a cluster of pills into my hand and popped them in my mouth; a few scrambled to safety, like bugs, but I got most of them. Then I swept up a handful of sea water and splashed it into my mouth. It wasn't good but it was drinkable. I took another handful of pills, another handful of water, then I dumped the rest down my throat. I had to sit very still to make sure I didn't throw up.

Then I looked around. It seemed the sky had opened wide for me. You could hear the lapping against the side of the canoe. I felt myself getting sleepy, I heard a fish splash, a few bars of music drifted from a hotel patio way, way across the water. The old couple danced on the patio, the waiter closing up now, putting away the bottles under the bar.

Quand il me prend dans ses bras
Il me parle tout bas,
Je vois la vie en rose . . .

I lay down in the boat, the stars blinking and blinking and blinking. I took a deep breath. I could feel my body slowing down; how lovely it was out here on the water, how reassuring. I closed my eyes, and after a while my thoughts, like people lying motionless on the floor, suddenly got up and moved about on their own.

I saw my mother in her red scarf, and my dentist and poor Johnny Best from across the street. They were leaning over the canoe, looking down at me. Somebody whispered, "Squeeze in, folks, squeeze in." I saw my boss and a policeman I didn't recognize. There's the woman from the bank with her hair tucked behind her ears. Shy smiles, strangers rubbing shoulders with strangers. There's my grade five teacher. "This is the universe, Roman," he says, "and these are the four levels of human experience." There's the baby who was crying on the plane today, and Aunt Minnie, who died in her sleep; even that intern I had a crush on years ago. Everyone squeezing together. And Jessica Zippin, thank God you've come, no hard feelings, Jessica taking the barrette from her hair and shaking it loose. "I'm more interesting this way," she says.

More arrivals, late arrivals, better late than never, a girl in an Indian shirt (I can't quite place her), my camp counsellor—my God, how many people make up a life. Oh look, there's Simon when he was just a toddler, look at him stumbling across the lawn in his diaper, plump little arms. My mother gently rocking the canoe, *Star light, star bright, first star I see tonight.* I could feel the boat slowly turn toward the open sea. Drifting and drifting and drifting all the way to China.

13

_____

It must have been afternoon when I woke up. The canoe bumped against a core of dead coral. A sailboat plopped by not fifty yards away. I could hear the sheet flapping in the wind. A woman in a lawn chair waved at me from the deck; she was wearing a red hat, pushing it down on her head so it didn't blow away in the wind. She shouted something at me, it sounded like Portuguese.

There was a green mess in the bottom of the boat, flies buzzing around it; I must have thrown up in the night. I raised my head over the gunnel. The jungle swam sickeningly. I got out of the boat—the coral stung my feet—and started up the bank. It was thick bush, very hot and damp, and I grabbed at branches and small trees to pull myself up. Finally I got to the top. A white road ran down the side of the island. I looked up and down, no vehicles, no houses. But the sun was too hot, nauseatingly hot, and I threw up again in the shade, on all fours. I lay in a ball, my eyes closed, and I imagined being on the yacht with the woman in the red hat, that she had taken me belowdecks and was pouring me a drink of water. But every time I put out my hand to take the glass, she dumped the water back in the sink. "Just a second," she said. "Wait till it's cold."

I said, "It's fine, really, the way it is," but she said, "Hang on, just a second longer," holding the glass under the faucet.

I fell asleep again, the pills floating like syrup in my blood. The air cooled. I heard a car stop; three voices, all men, standing over me. "Il est crevé, non?" He's had it.

Someone rolled me over. I could feel them going through my pockets. I didn't open my eyes. They took off my belt. I lay very still, hiding in my cocoon. Hiding way down there.

"Foutons-le-camp." I heard the car start up and take off, then stop, as if they had had second thoughts. But then they drove away.

It was after dark when I woke up a second time. I started down the white road, staggering this way and that. Never so thirsty, but not a house in sight. I saw a lighthouse way down the road. I thought, I know that lighthouse, but I couldn't remember from where. I kept on; the jungle creaked and chirped with creatures just out of sight; a moon rose again in the sky as if hauled up on a pulley. I kept walking and walking, thinking, I have to get something to drink. I was coming around a gentle corner when I saw, just ahead of me, a yellow house. I heard a tinkle; a small boy was standing on the porch shielding his eyes from a naked light bulb. I waved, I hurried, shoeless, toward him, but he went inside.

I caught up to the house and stood at the base of the stairs, just inside the rim of light. A wind chime tinkled over the door. I could hear a television. A soccer game. I went up the rough wooden stairs and knocked on the door. I said, "Excuse me." There was no answer.

I knocked again, harder. I said, "Excuse me, I'm terribly thirsty, may I come in?"

Then I went in.

I want to thank my new editor and publisher, Patrick Crean, for buying the book and then persuading me to throw it away and start over. I want to thank the waiters at Le Paradis restaurant for their elegance and their indulgence; also Maggie Huculak, Dennis Lee, Daniel Richler, John McClelland, Barbara Kennedy, Paula Kirman, Iaian Greenson, Maggie Gilmour, George Maxwell, Nigel Dickson, David Reed, Heydon Park, Random House (for years of patience), the Ontario Arts Council, Michael Flaxman for lessons in the art of bank robbery; and, of course, I want to thank my son, Jesse Gilmour, for his courageous and astute criticism on *this* side of the river.

)